John Albee

Prose Idyls

John Albee

Prose Idyls

ISBN/EAN: 9783743305335

Manufactured in Europe, USA, Canada, Australia, Japa

Cover: Foto ©Andreas Hilbeck / pixelio.de

Manufactured and distributed by brebook publishing software
(www.brebook.com)

John Albee

Prose Idyls

PROSE IDYLS

BY

JOHN ALBEE

BOSTON AND NEW YORK
HOUGHTON, MIFFLIN AND COMPANY
The Riverside Press, Cambridge
1892

The Riverside Press, Cambridge, Mass., U. S. A.
Electrotyped and Printed by H. O. Houghton & Co.

TO

E. A. AND L. S. A.

CONTENTS

PROSE IDYLS

WHITE THOUGHTS

THE young maiden looks out between the curtains of her window in the early morning before she is half dressed.

She is still nearly all in white ; her lips and cheeks are flushed with joyous dreams ; and, luminous under her marble brow, they resemble the pink blossoms of the arbutus among its white sisters.

She looks out of the window and sees the earth buried in snow. The roofs are covered with a white thatch that bends under the eaves like a giant's hands curled up with the cold. The trees, too, bear great plumes of snow at the extreme ends of their branches ; they hang almost to the ground with the weight. The sky itself is no longer blue ; it is the color of milk.

Why should winter and cold clothe themselves always in such pale robes ? mused the maiden. Even the winter sun is white.

She resumes her dressing.

But her thoughts look out of the window. The snow-robed earth makes her think of weddings, of brides, of the long satin train, the white veil coming down almost to the feet and flowing over the head like a mist. Her cheeks grow more rosy.

Then she thinks of the dead in their winding-sheets ; the same whiteness, the pale face, the blanched lips, death's pallor, which is but an extinguished white ; the shroud almost as long and full as a bridal dress.

Why should love and death alike be decked in white ? she mused. Is it then only that we become wholly pure ?

Then she completes her toilet. But she lingers as having forgotten something. She draws the curtains wide apart and gazes long, out upon the milky sky, upon the snow glittering in the sun like an immense tapestry wrought with pearls and diamonds.

Once more she returns to the mirror, as if she had just remembered something.

She selects the whitest flower from her lover's bouquet and arranges it over her bosom.

She thinks no more of the white winter, the buried earth, the pallid ghosts. It is summer in her heart.

I own a thousand trees ; yes, a forest — a forest that extends from the mountain to the valley which opens into the world.

My trees, full of leafiness and sweet with unnamed perfumes, reflect their gigantic shadows in the lake ; they softly wave their topmost sprays before the inexorable blue doors of the sky, down there in that silent, silver mirror.

Yet because of Helen's trees mine no longer satisfy me. Hers she has named with names she loves. Mine stand nameless ; and futile it is for them to shoot upward, or flaunt a bolder instep as their feet sink deeper beneath the moss-covered mould. You shall be cut down, you nameless ones, if you continue thus vainly to grow ;

nor shall the duplicity of your images in the lake flatter me any longer; and as you have no names, you shall not be remembered; nor shall the Dryads shriek as you fall, for they dwell not in my forest. The subtle-minded Helen has shepherded them all into hers; and Diana hunts there, and Pan pipes, and even the bears from the mountain she has made welcome.

I, alas! never remembered the divinities, nor did I name any tree after the goddesses whom I adore. Deftly I trained them, lopping away the lower limbs for unwished light, unminded of the wonted retreats of the timid satyrs and the fauns that love to crop the tender, shaded sprouts. So I made all like a park, wherein men walk who fear beasts and are in dread to meet the wood nymphs. And I bethought me of all the manifold uses of the trunks of my trees, when they should be scarfed by the woodman's axe; I rejoiced when I saw them shorn and hewn and forever imprisoned under my feet and over my head.

Now, alas! the beams of my house afflict me like ghosts, and they wave long supplicating or deprecatory arms toward me, even as yonder winter-worn trees toss their baffled branches in the windy night against the cold and rigid stars.

I will retract all my thoughts of the utilities of my forest; for Helen's trees are not beams; their august spires touch the heavens — the Uranian heavens which Pan and all the Muses gave to her when they consecrated her groves. Too late — too late I saw the good of disuse and unprofitableness.

And I envy them their names. But I cannot do what another has done. Neither can anything be done twice that is beautiful; and my trees may outgrow and overtop hers — they will still be common trees.

I know what I will do, I will dis-

own them ; and even the white birches
that stand at the portal of my forest,
like brides coming out of their chambers, shall have cause to weep for neg-
lect.

It is because of Helen's trees that I
weary of the long wooded slopes with
their undulating dark green waves, the
trim spruces and glossy hemlocks, an
indistinguishable assemblage ; they fill
me with languor like the salons of the
city.

I will go and walk among Helen's
trees, and perchance I shall divine
which one it was she signified and
named for me. If I cannot find it,
surely it will beckon to me with its
friendly arms. It does not idly reflect itself against the counterfeit sky
imprisoned in the lake, nor swing in
every wind, but like her soul it is agi-
tated by the breath of the celestial
sphere.

Come, Helen, sing that song of thine,
under the beech-tree which thou hast

named for me, for now I have found upon the bark the postil of thy hand; and thy band of maidens shall join their undersong ; while I, voiceless, contemplate with silent scorn, such as no other poet ever felt before for his own possessions, my herd of unlettered oaks and inarticulate pines.

WITH the sweetness of a flower that has just unfolded itself for the first time in the spring of the year, the maiden Launa smiled ; and at that moment I chanced to stand where her smile fell upon me. After that moment chance was no more the procuress of smiles.

To mortals the destinies appear but once, for an instant. In their fleet, impalpable passages over the earth they enter only portals already opened ; but carefully do they close and bar them, once entered.

I lived a thousand years ; I became gray as the Theban Apollo. My skin was like an ancient palimpsest, and my bones rattled like chips upon a floor. Launa Probana smiled upon me, and I arose from my ruins with the vigor and vivacity of a boy. Such was I, Nicban, the companion of Launa, before the world was, before the double stars had selected their mates ; such I continue through the ages.

Hear me, O gray Theban Apollo ! I will tell you of our life upon the earth, since thou knowest that before, and that which shall be.

Mortals are not as they seem even in the first years. We had knowledge even then ; but we had not then, nor ever after, the wish to reveal it, no, not even to each other ; and we passed among other mortals as children needing instruction and the tuition of the elder bards.

Under the long rows of elms we went hand in hand to the schools for children ; we stood side by side before the magicians appointed to unfold our minds ; their charms, their miracles could not deceive us. We read from the same page that which we already knew. If there was anything dark, or

if I became languid from the sum of
the ignorance continually presupposed
for us, Launa's smile restored me; and
the same serene light appeared in my
soul as when I first stood in its pathway.

If there was knowledge, we knew it
when we arrived at it; and what we
learned, O Apollo, from thy chosen
ones, that we became, Launa first and
I not long afterwards. Or if there
were then such things as wisdom and
beauty beyond the walls that men
build to confine them, beyond the
tomes of the sages and the experiences
of hoary ancestors, these we drank in
at many a hidden fountain.

In the morning we gathered flowers;
at noontide we exchanged the fruits of
the earth prepared for each of us. In
the afternoon, prone upon the hillside
under the young birches, we sailed
with the high, translucent cloudlets,
or sent messages by them to the evening stars. In secret places we built

houses of boughs and roofs of brake, not large enough for company, nor pleasant enough for more than one day. These now, later generations of children discover as the seats of a remote and extinct civilization.

Under the low arched bridge we waded among the ripples, and under them saw our bare feet become as large as those of our elders. The friendly spiders looked down from the roof, and water-flies gave over their perpetual gyrations and watched us with delight. I carried Launa over many a brook at whose depth she pretended to be affrighted. Did she wish to feel her arms around my neck? You know, ye blessed gods, who knew the heart of Launa Probana. But I knew it not. Clasping her firmly and stepping cautiously among the reeds and peplis, I felt only the emotion, the agitation of a hero.

Together we explored the further side of every stream, hill, wood; for was it not there that the mystery, the secret lurked which we were perpetually looking for?—the secret which only allured us to the next.

Thus did we come afresh to the apprehension of the myths of the olden times, which penumbrate divine beings and their thoughts. To us they dissembled not, but took us by the hand and disclosed to us the arcana of forest and waters and mountain pinnacles ; and we became like-minded, and held intercourse with such of their company as yet retained remembrance of their mortal state, doomed for yet awhile to the condition of demigods. From them we learned to be silent and impassive when we approached that which was in its inner being divine.

Ever as before, this too seemed but the intuition of our own souls ; for never had we spoken of ourselves to each other, while drawing more and more near. Thy smile, Launa Probana, smote across rooms, between the faces of friends and comrades, over fields and waters, through a thousand years, and communicated to me the whole of life and the path of immortality. The bow of thy lips encompassed me. And whether our breath made frost figures on the same window pane, or whether, leaning over the rail of the boat, we beheld our faces in the shouldering waves run into one, we understood these as the emblem of that which was, which had been, and which would be forever.

GRAMMARIAN IN LOVE

Who knows when he is wholly in love? Not I. My mother said I was in love with Candide; and I believed it myself.

For a long time my mother had wished me to find a bride. She said I was getting dusty like my books, that we both needed some one to brush us up and keep us from moths — moths she calls them, experienced housewife as she is; she knows not the little creature that vermiculates the choicest passages in my rarest tomes. Those tomes, I was already wedded to them.

Yet when I beheld Candide's white teeth and the rubicund curve of her lips, and heard her voice that trebled like a bird's, I forgot study.

Hand in hand we studied nature.

Candide's voice trebled like a bird's, among flowers, in the groves, over brooks and meadows where the cowslip enamels her six sepals and her luxuriant leaves alike.

How dusty are books! thought I. "Were it not better done as others use?" kept ringing in my ears.

And Candide's voice trebled like a bird's. I heard it now when alone. Nay, we did not permit each other to be alone ; and others — there were none! We indulged ourselves in the egoism of two.

Only there was nature, on which we threw ourselves, like the alchemist's last projection, and changed all to gold.

Silent, patient nature! What metamorphoses hast thou to bear from lovers, what flatteries! Didst thou, too, hear Candide's trebling voice and believe it one of thine own? Dost thou never weary of the monotonies of thine external iterations from bird and wind and water and leaves? And, ah me, from thy bards?

Candide trebled on. When she was not talking she was singing, and at length I could not distinguish one from the other. In any case the words were of no moment in my ears. I heard only a certain music, of which I thought I should never tire. Does one tire of a street song, filtered down from I know not where — the grand opera, perhaps?

I was the first to hear her voice; it was not the world's yet. And the words — we never mind them ; we make them to suit the instant emotion.

Nevertheless, one evil day I brought my bird to book.

We left nature, her mossy seats and pillows, her leafy branches, and bowers too large for one, her hilltops, and heaven over all, and we sat down in chairs — the chairs, alas! of this underworld.

The treble of Candide's voice diminished, grew broken, sober, embarrassed.

It tried to speak in my language. I had had no difficulty in being silent in hers. Here now we sat in chairs, decorous like those in other chairs, conversing in something called speech, prose, strict, intelligible, the terrible dialect of this under-world, which I, like a galley slave, am doomed to clank about in, while I hear afar off the speech of Candide's native realm, its long vowels, its words of benediction that raise the heart and put reason to sleep. Fool that I was! to think that Candide's treble could be confined in four walls and a chair, and attested by my learned tomes of ancient and uninspired sages. Fool! that I should wish my humming-bird to alight like another, and to speak as my books, without solecisms and tautologies. What is love but never-ending tautology? So much grammar and Candide have taught me. But no one had taught Candide; no, not even I.

Alas! now the dust settles upon my

books and upon me, and my mother is hopeless. But Candide goes trebling through the world ; she is happy, and she will never learn grammar. Would that I might again hear her voice, though in a solecism.

I listen ; all is so still here among voices that once made such a stir. I listen — I hear only the little creatures vermiculating the vellum of Philostratus at his twenty-fourth letter. Ah, the epicures ! How well they scent the good things !

PAIN AND PLEASURE

WE were begotten twins of a mother who, having suffered more than mortal anguish, expired at our birth with excess of joy.

We were separated as soon as we were brought forth. Thenceforth pursuing each other through the worlds and among the spaces of the most distant stars, never have we been reunited for a single instant, but where one came the other had just departed.

Well we know each other's trail, paved with pearls that once were tears and bordered with stems once in bloom, undeviating, ever returning upon itself; and our camps are never wanting the presence of one or other of us. The signal of departure is the signal of arrival.

The monotony of our journeyings

would be more wearisome, but that as guests we are sometimes mistaken one for the other. In the house of lovers we are often thus confounded, and in the chambers of first-born babes. In the house of music also the inmates are never certain which to call us ; because, in truth, under some mysterious conditions our natures become interchangeable, and tears and smiles are but false criterions.

In the houses of poets we seldom remain long enough at one time to be identified. It is through them we make our quickest yet most frequent flights ; so that if any one should find either heralded there, let him not be too confident ; it is as likely to be the other. But the poets sometimes boast that we are indistinguishable, and give us equal welcome, equal praise.

There is only one abode we avoid — where more than mortal fortitude is professed ; where hang our pretended portraits in a portico devoted to moderate pleasures and majestic pains. The Stoics believe not in us, and we reciprocate their skepticism. For the time is not yet when men can know themselves without a knowledge of both of us.

Nature makes the lives of most animals brief as a compensation for all that they endure from their masters, and also because they can make little use of the experience gained of us.

It is I, the twin brother of Pleasure, that dictate this memorial by the hand of my intimate. I surrender for some years the lives of children and many youths and maids to my brother, knowing that in due season they will be subjected to me. If by chance they escape, I await the moment when such blessed beings, departing hence, will leave me the procession which follows them to the tomb. I claim tribute in the last and usually in the first breath of all that exists. Thus everywhere and at all times is our sovereignty divided in a just division.

Men testify that this is not the truth, and that some are always my victims and others the life-long favorites of my brother. They know not that where the seed of one is planted, it bears not its own fruit but that of the other. As night follows the day, as tides ebb and flow, as season gives place to season, so do we follow each other in the life of man that he may be fitted for final repose.

But well do I know that I am mortal, and that at last I shall be overtaken, dissolved, and lost in the glorious being of my immortal brother.

THE CRACKED BELL

IT is a breach of manners to enter late a Protestant service. At a Catholic you drop on your knees, you are forgiven, you stand where you are, or go boldly forward to your seat.

In my village the Protestant bell was cracked; it did not send its call as far as was its wont, and the punctual Margaret was late. Others began to be; in short, it came about that all were late, even the clergyman. For on the Sabbath no one trusts his own watch; he waits to hear the bell. It is the Sentinel of Heaven.

But it was cracked, and souls were in danger.

As if in sympathy with the bell, its tower was rent; howbeit, the bell fell not; there it hung almost by a splinter.

They rang it no more; some said it

would widen the crack, others that it would bring down the tower, even to toll it.

People now came to church according to the time of their several watches and clocks; some midway of the services, some almost at the close; others did not come at all. It was the fault of the bell; yes, every one said it was the fault of the bell.

By some strange accident the mind of the clergyman was beclouded and changed; he knew not what to think or speak for fear of leading his flock away from heaven. He no longer delivered with authority simple and impressive precepts. They were colored and lengthened by various beautiful but uncertain lights.

The forlorn people now came to church according to their several inclinations; some from habit, some for a walk, some with nothing else to do; most came not at all. It was the fault of the bell; yes, all confessed it was the fault of the bell in the beginning, and now another evil had befallen, the clergyman's voice, that, too, gave an uncertain sound.

An old woman, who had enjoyed and suffered the entire fortunes of life, continued to come at the appointed hour. She was partly deaf ; she could not have heard the bell, even when not cracked. She did not know that it hung by a splinter. She was simple, and though in a front pew, she could not have understood the subtle doubts of her clergyman ; she only came to worship God !

And when alone of all the congregation she was left the sole worshiper, the bell suddenly sounded forth its ancient clear call, the rent tower closed, the clergyman himself forgot his doubts.

THE MIND CURER

It would be well, said the sage to me one day, to go to college; it would be better to go round the world; but best of all to go look everything thou meetest with in the face and ask of it some question that is in thine own heart. If thou art patient, but withal importunate, then after many years thou wilt find the answers written everywhere, in a pre-Cadmean alphabet — such were his very words — over all waste places and in the dust under thy feet.

Thus spoke the sage, and many other things of similar import, speaking like the Pythoness across the centuries, regardless of age, time, and circumstances.

As I had gone clandestinely, had hired a chaise and traveled twenty

miles at the expense of all my sub-
stance to consult the oracle, I held it
to be mine, and I treasured it up for
many years without comprehending
it.   Yet generally I felt it, like Soc-
rates' demon, restraining me from
many things.   I know not how, but the
lofty words and their very vagueness
elevated the soul and made it expectant of wonderful revelations.   If I
sought honor, ease, riches, love, something said, Seek them not! and at
length they palled before a life, not
mine, but whose existence I could
divine.   As the astronomer knows of
an unseen star by the perturbations
of some other visible, so I conjectured
of a higher life by the agitations, the
attractions and repulsions of this.

Thus did the sage and the master of
many centuries cure the uncertain,
adolescent mind ere yet it had reached
to follies or prevented the entrance of
wisdom.

CREATION

I HAVE long envied the sculptor who, through extreme fondness, brought a soul into his statue. It is wonderful, but not improbable. All good statues desire to come to life. It happens often. It happens as often as there is a conjunction of genius with the requisite skill. Then is given life and immortality under the material tissues, under the semblances which art invents in marble, on paper and on canvas.

I also, like Pygmalion, have worshiped the work of my own hands; and that which I passionately loved, working upon it with the whole force of my nature, in seclusion, without ambition, without emulation or rewards, has often become a living thing, and returned with gratitude and affection the effort or the prayer which gave to it release from the prison house of matter.

Thus have I surrounded myself with a family of children. The great artist has need of no other instrument than his imagination. What he imagines leaps into existence full-formed, only requiring nurture and culture, which the dexterity of his art is already prepared to supply.

There they stand or sit, my children, obedient to my most inexpressible thought, until I give them their freedom by some magic word, for which I and they alike await in silence and expectancy. Then at length I exclaim, "Awake, advance, live!"

But it is also true that I am incommoded by many half-formed, inchoate, yes, even mal-formed beings. They will neither allow themselves to be remanded to the void, to nothingness, nor will they take the one step which I urge, which I demand with loud voice and upraised, threatening quill, the one step from seeming to being, from sleep and dream to animation and self - existence. There they sit dumb in the corner, like a guest who has been somehow invited, but whom you know not how to entertain. The worst of it is that they take up too much room in a house so small as mine.

Shall I also confess that sometimes even those creations which have attained to a life of their own, and are capable of mobility, will not separate themselves from my household, but hover about and afflict me with terrible tedium and melancholy ? Is it possible they can find no other home, that no one will receive and adopt them ?

If so, they should not have lived ; for what is the good of a family of children whom you cannot send out into the world to better it, and perchance themselves, but who must always remain in the nest, unfledged, with no note, no voice, no song, strictly their own ?

NOT to-day, nor yesterday, but in an unremembered time, lived a man who was an unconscious poet. He possessed also, and much in the same way, a great estate ; nevertheless he dwelt in one little corner of it.

Far away, on the extreme confines of his domain, arose the peak of a lofty mountain. It was so distant and so blue that he thought it was a part of the sky. He never dreamed it was his ; he never attempted to explore the summit ; least of all did it occur to him to make any use of his Parnassian mountain pastures. Others herded their fat flocks there, and piped and sang after the manner of fortunate and happy shepherds.

All the while he enjoyed contemplating it ; that alone made him happy and blest; made him dear to all folks; and more beloved by his friends and the gods of his own mountain.

No one knew he was a poet, although all who had intercourse with him immediately became poets. No one who saw him plodding about his obscure little corner suspected that his estate inclosed the very summit of the mountain, so distant and so blue that it was scarcely distinguishable from the heavens.

Down deep in his soul, behind a thin but impenetrable veil, hid the poet; and every one went on believing he knew all about the gentle and friendly neighbor dwelling contentedly in his little corner under the high stars.

In those impitiable eyes I beheld no retraction of her disdainful, taciturn words ; and methought under her purple fillet shot forth little resilient tongues of flames, like those that escape from the wheels of an electric car.

Beware ! they seemed to hiss, those viperous, sleided tongues of poisonous fire. Beware I could not, and I would not. And that which threatened to destroy enticed me on with threefold enchantment.

One devil casts out another in the infernal comedy of my life. For I no longer breathed the bacchanal air of self-flattery and of an egoism high as the dome of the sky which I had seemed to touch, where I neither permitted nor perceived any other existence than my own.

She, it was she who had dethroned me, and filled up the universe with herself and her sorceries. Thus thrust out my heaven, more false than that fabled of brass, I fell — fell into the sea, the insatiable sea of her being ; until with the surrender of self-love I was abandoned to a soul so like my own in its egoism, but being woman's so far surpassing man's as the subtlety of her nature exceeds his, that I was at last destroyed by it. Yet I lived on, conscious, unresistingly conscious, that in slavery to her I was ministering to the same devil that formerly possessed myself.

Yes ; in the infernal comedy of false love there are two players, but a single part.

A REMINISCENCE OF VIRGIL

I OPENED the grammar at the wrong place. Surely the exception was there; but I could not find the one that Master Virgil has so adroitly slipped into the verse, just to plague a schoolboy.

Let it go, said I ; it will come in some other fellow's passage.

" Sir, you may sit! you do not understand it ;" and the great Professor's eyes, raised just above his spectacles, dropped back behind them again like two bullets, as he called up from the bench of trembling boys the next protagonist.

What a bad thing is the Latin grammar !

He had also to sit down, overwhelmed with shame.

This time the Professor did not speak ; he only raised his eyes above the

square, gold-bowed spectacles, and re-
fracting their powerful dioptric glasses
methought I detected a faint line of
blue light, like a strand of fading rain-
bow, or the nether fringe of a thunder
cloud, under which the horizon strug-
gles against extinction.

This time, but more emphatically,
he dropped them like two bullets ; and
the champion of the class, he who
knew every exception, fell back into
his seat as if the battle were lost.

The battle was lost ; we were in
confusion and retreat ; the little we
knew fled through the windows, rushed
out of the doors, ran up the chimney,
and the fourth book of the Æneid was
lost, buried deeper than vanquished
Troy.

What then ! did not Master Virgil
compose those beautiful cæsuras to
discipline us in grammar — that we
might become expert grammarians ?

But for all that I loved Master Virgil. I loved him when I read the

Bucolics under a tree, and also when I recited his heroics to my brothers, the drapers and tanners.

Ah, you will divine why; I did not construe them very well, and I had forgotten paradigms and exceptions, and most of all that most erudite of grammatistical Professors who threw out of the window the flowers of the Æneid.

For all that, I felt only the happiness of shepherds and shepherdesses; the Saturnian age and the sufferings of heroes.

I forgot even short syllables and long, and those voluptuous words and blushing tropes which nibbed such a salacious pen for Montaigne, as he ambled up and down his sixteen-paced tower.

THE BIRD SANG

A LITTLE bird sang to me from her gilded cage, hung in the top of the window.

She sang, but I could not catch her words ; notwithstanding, as in some strange human speech, half knowing what it wishes to say, so I knew not the words of the little songster, but I comprehended her meaning.

She sang, and this was her song : " Water and seeds have I enough ; and a fig and a pale green lettuce leaf ; a hoop to swing, and one above another three perches ; on one I sleep and on one I eat and on this I sing. But, ah me ! my cage is so round, and I never come by the end of it. Round and round and still the same ! Never a corner, never a covert from observation ; never shade nor recess whither

I may fly and hide — I who love seclusion and sometimes not to be seen,
even when I sing.

" There is no place of retreat, save
when I put my head under my wing
and dream that I am alone. I should
better like a square cage, whose limits
would not seem so hopeless and mo-
notonous as this wearisome circle ; or
one like many-storied houses with lock
and curtain ; or as the dog's kennel,
where he sleeps and ruminates ; or
like that of my brother, the caged
squirrel, that has a cave in which, if
he only imagines he hides himself, he
seems happy.

" But this inclosure — is it meant to
resemble your world, to simulate freedom and be still a prison ? "

Then I pondered ; and I answered
the song of the little bird as much as
I could : " No, little bird ; thy song is
sweet, and sweet even thy complaint.
But there are no more any corners in
the world ; no more any seclusions ; no

more any privacies. Alas! the world was created round like thy cage, although not in its present rotundity; but every day it grows rounder. There was a time when it was even flat, and men of old days walked to the end of it and touched the sky. O happy men! But now all is seen, all without moving is revealed; there is no longer any secret place. As through the bars of thy gilded cage, we peer into each other's unfenceless world. The human eye has become akin to God's. There is no more any escape for thee and me. As thou puttest thy head under thy wing as a last refuge from sight, so do I withdraw my soul only from the gaze of the world.

"My cage is round and open on all sides like thine. Sometimes, too, it is gilded; sometimes it is black as the bars at the entrance of tombs. But always it is on all sides like thine; like the earth round and round; and like the earth worn slowly down, everything that dares thrust itself beyond the indomitable circle. And evermore equality, monotony, mediocrity, publicity, rejoice over their conquests.

" Like the spheres, we touch but do not meet ; there is no longer need of meeting, since all are all alike and all is visible, as in a house of glass ; and windows are set in the inmost mansions of men. My dearest friend already knows what I am about to say to her ; she has divined it, she has said it ! We know each other so well ! all know all. Youth knows as much as age, and age knows no more. The world is round and rounder, and all things grow plain. Light irradiates the invisible, the mysterious, the visionary. Color has faded away from the human panorama, crowded with etiolated cosmopolites.

" Thou dear illusionist, wonder-eyed, credulous, singing gladsome strains of gods and heroes to their progeny, the men of ancient days, go hence ; thy world is broken, there is no room for thee.

"And thou, little prisoner in thy gilded cage, sing thy song and thy plaint; and when thou wouldst be alone, put thy head beneath thy wing, as I withdraw my soul, my soul only, from the ever-advancing myrmidons."

I WAS standing before Murillo's Madonna. Twice have I traveled afar to see it. This was the second time.

I stood now a long time before the Madonna, trying hard to raise the vision of my soul where I might look down into her upturned eyes. She would not suffer it, although I raised myself to the pinnacle of heaven.

Then I said, conscious of my just repulse, " Thou art well worthy to be the Mother of a God!"

I turned at the echo of my words, but they died away along the sides of the gallery and from behind many admirable pictures.

Silence is better in this presence, thought I.

Once more I turned my gaze upon the Madonna's face.

But now, letting my eyes wander, I saw other faces in the painting, cherubs, angels of infancy, nascent forms, from which the promised God was to be chosen.

Even as I thought this I heard their sweet infantine tones imploring the expectant Mother to be taken to her embrace.

Then knew I why those eyes upturned to heaven, beyond mortal response; and why those hands clasped tightly her bosom, as yet clasping nothing.

For they were appealing to the Lord of Heaven, those looks, those arms, not for her own choice, but his.

And as I looked now steadfastly in a new knowledge, the lot was cast, the choice made.

Under her arms was the Child, and her eyes looked down into mine and into those of all the world, filling them with joy.

O HAPPY days of the March town-
meeting, ere the boy is a man and a
maker of laws ! Happy days ! when
one goes to the polls, but does not
vote. This theme, at least, was never
before attempted in song.

Come, teach me the measure, muse
of Ascra and the Catonian farm. For
never could I in a straight course
round the stake of the sonnet fourteen
times and barely reach the goal ; nor
with my rustic lyre swing in song like
a bird from tree to tree without once
flapping a heavy wing ; nor yet could
my short arm wield the hypermeters
of Walt Whitman, that stretch across
the page like a prairie furrow.

Not Athens, nor Alexandria, nor
Lutetia can teach me ; but my masters
shall come from Beotian ploughlands,

from oldest Aryan fields, the wattled Saxon acre, the stone walls and red houses of New England.

Come, then, all ye rural muses that sit so prim and plain on the roofs and belfries of all the little town-houses and meeting-houses of my native land : come! and I will sing the song of freedom learned on jewsharp and whistle, turned now to triumphant trumpet and drum, while I, a white-handed poet, am proud to march with the myrmidons of democracy. But chiefly my voice is heard in the March town-meeting and in the annals of my island home. There, like Ulysses, I have ever cared more for Penelope than fame, and all my nurture was derived from the school, the farm and the town-meeting.

We played about the houses of freedom ; we heard the voices within ; we saw the stern faces of our fathers as they went to and fro. We entered the aisles and listened. Leaning on rail and post we beheld the little state in motion. Speech was brief ; it was awkward and slow ; intention and action were clear as the noon and strong as mountains. The fathers arose ; with one upward swing of their hands they made schools, churches, the pound, the train-band, the house for the poor. Then for a year they rested ; then they assembled again ; and after many years the great King and all the world knew the meaning of the town-meeting. But too late ! We too were kings !

On the second Tuesday of March we make ridiculous the pomposities and bombast of senates and forums. We open the meeting without ceremonial, and before the day is done we have regulated the calendar of the year, and gone home to live it out. The recusants, although they swear and scoff, will abide by it.

The boys play about the doors of the house of freedom until it is time for them to enter and take the places allotted them below their elders, and learn to vote and to act. But until that time they play about the door. And on that March Tuesday, the great secular Sabbath of the yeomen, with twenty-five cents, the savings of a whole winter, the boy is richer and happier than when he owns a farm and yokes his own oxen. For a month before he deliberates on what he shall buy — for twenty-five cents will buy so many things when one is twelve years old! Not until the very day and after his arrival does he settle on three buns, some sticks of striped and twisted candy, and an imitation cigar made of dark sugar with a fiery end. At the other end of that cigar he mocks the jaunty manners of elder boys. He swaggers and pretends to spit. A red and tingling ear reminds him that he is only twelve. He eats a bun and is himself again.

When the day is done, the year is

over for him.   A few more such years
and the boy is twenty-one; he receives his majority steers, the gift of
his father, and a freedom suit, the gift
of his mother, spun, woven and sewed
with her own hands.   Then he votes.
He sits with dignity through the pro-
ceedings of the town-meeting.   As
yet it is indecorous for him to take
an active part.   He silently votes; he
restrains the speech of his deep, atten-
tive mind.   In time he openly partici-
pates in the discussion, and he comes
into office, rising through lower grades
to be at last a selectman.

He who can boast a selectman as
an ancestor has a right to his pride,
and may quarter his arms with princes
and pontiffs.   For my part I cannot.
A road-surveyor is as high as I can go.
My father, mighty man with scythe
and axe, wrote a fair round hand, plain
as print, which was thought to qualify
him to be the town clerk; and my
grandfather was celebrated for doing

hard sums with chalk on the backs of bellows. But luck passed them by; and I am but the plebeian dregs of a road-surveyor and rustic arithmetician. Bran and meal come off the same cob.

Yet humble as we are who only vote others into office, we know the "Town's Mind." This phrase, invented by our forefathers, shows their closeness to their own affairs. It is a drop from an imperial cup ; it is the large, assumptive "We" of kings and Elohims, brought hither and written over the portals of all dwellings, churches, school-houses, town-houses, of the smallest community.

Wonderful is it how well we can manage our own affairs — we who are not lawyers or statesmen ; we who know little of grammar, the nominative case or the previous question. Four or five figures is the maximum of our arithmetic and our expenses. All this we do in plain houses of wood, without architecture or the statue of any god.

But the God who watches over plain, brave men is not far off, and to Him I dedicate my song; and I invoke his power to preserve this low-roofed citadel of the free.

THE STATUE OF MY FRIEND

MORE precious than fine gold was the man whom I called my dearest friend.

When he died I was too poor to bury him in that state which he deserved and which I desired. Nor could I afford an artist to perpetuate in marble or upon canvas his figure, glorious as a shaft of sunlight when it strikes the highest dome of Bagdad or Damascus. Yet I feared to lose him if I trusted only to the slowly fading tablet of memory; for fade alike the dearest and most indifferent images, and the misery of life is that trifles involuntarily present themselves in the memory, after some lapse of time, with as much vividness as those things which we desire should alone remain in our hearts.

I resolved to keep my friend just as he was in life, as I could not afford a fitting tomb for him, nor retain him in marble nor yet upon canvas.

I betook myself to my ancient acquaintance, the alchemist, Ben Hassam, and confiding to him the condition of my purse and my wishes, he, out of friendliness and sympathy, freely offered his arts, which would enable me to keep possession of my friend to the end of my days.

"Yes," said Ben Hassam, "I will preserve for you the bodily form in every lineament, slightly darkened in color, but do not expect me to bring back the spirit. Allah has now emptied that into some other receptacle. Mortals must be content, when friends take the long journey in the caravans that cross the unknown desert, with the vessel which once held the wine of life.

"But come, let us proceed with our labor, first offering a prayer for our friend and then for ourselves." Which having done, Ben Hassam prepared all things necessary for the device of rendering immortal so much of my friend as was spared to me after the butterfly had ascended from his lips.

The processes of Ben Hassam were all, save one, simple, and all effective; I watched my friend issue from each successive stage nearer to life, nearer to himself in his most ideal condition of lovely form and perfect vigor. At every step I could hardly refrain from embracing him.

First we paint him with nitrate of silver; then with a vapor of white phosphorus render his skin dark and lustrous. We then dip him in an electric bath, depositing all over his splendid body a fine new cuticle, an epidermis of iridescent copper. This was the last of the chemical processes. The profound alchemical secrets of Ben Hassam which I could not penetrate now exerted themselves; but it was obvious that a layer of life-like integument completely enwrapped what was only a moment ago a poor wasted cadaver ; so that, like an athlete fresh from the strigil and the bath, he appears able once more to endure the shocks and outrages of the world. He feels no blow ; the stroke of dagger pierces him not.

It was now more than ever almost impossible to refrain from crying out and falling into his arms.

Only one more operation remained to complete the eternal preservation of the mortal part of my friend. In this the wonderful feature of Ben Hassam's skill revealed itself. All the previous efforts had been exercised to render the body externally not only as in life, but also impervious to every element. I felt that no blow, wind, rain, sun, frost, nor time itself could work him injury. I did not reckon with fire. What was my amazement to see, therefore, Ben Hassam proceed to incinerate my friend and consume every vestige of the internal mechanism of man without doing the least harm to the statue itself. This was the final device — a cleanly and complete exenteration, and the grosser portions departed whence they came.

At length all is over. We refresh ourselves with a little wine and a few olives from Ben Hassam's single tree, while we contemplate the work of our hands, the now perfect and imperishable statue of my friend, wrought not as others from stone and ivory, but from his own body, with feelings, I dare say, akin to those of the greatest artists.

SHE was poor, but there were others poorer. She thought herself rich because she had something she could do without, could share.

It is only the poor who can cross the road where Lazarus lies, yes, who would dare the great gulf between Abraham's bosom and the rich man's thirst. Over there in the Land of Misery is a half crust, never a whole one. The poor know that it is still possible to divide what has already been halved or quartered to them. This the rich see not. They give what is left. They never share the uncut loaf.

She stepped lightly across, always with a gift. She called it food, pieces of cloth, pins, a little thread, saved from the bastings of the garments

she sewed for those who made fortunes thereby; a half loaf, which she
learned to divide as others learn to
increase and multiply.

Her gift was in none of these; it
was herself she gave. You must ask
him who receives the value of the gift,
not the giver. Over there they never
mentioned what she brought to them,
but they passed it by and spoke of
her; and they called her " The Child
of God."

How did they know such good
words? how invent so majestic a
name?

It was not the hunger of the stom-
ach, nor the cold of the shoulders, nor
the overwork for merciless wages to
which she ministered that most
affected them. For these, the common hand of charity, the dole of a
thousand agencies, sufficed. It was
herself in her kindness, which they
distinguished from every other sort
of almsgiving. Neither cold nor star-

vation nor merciless wages had extinguished in their bosoms the image of
goodness, and they divined its bright
reflection in her whom they named
" The Child of God."

THE FAITH CURER

ONCE I knew a Child of God, and I told her story to those who had ears to hear.

Another one I knew, but she did not bear the same name. There was no one to give her a title, for her work was done in secret, moved by the pity she felt for sufferers, whom she had no earthly means of compassionating.

It was a long way up to her one room, nearer the sky than the earth. She was a tailoress, in the days when there was such a trade. She had no husband or child. She liked not men save when they were in distress, and she could not bear to be reminded of them at any other time. This was the reason why she preferred to cut and sew boys' clothing. That of men with its superserviceable pockets and flaps and

ever multiplying button holes gave her
thoughts a disagreeable and sometimes
almost disdainful turn. For little boys
she had a tenderness ; she stitched her
heart into their short breeches and
round jackets. She loved to see them
when she took their suits home to
try on.

Her room had nothing in it to de-
scribe beyond a cot, a table, a Bible,
and the few implements of her trade.
Her life seemed as narrow and unem-
bellished as her rooms. She had never
known those good words " take, have
and keep." There was nothing to envy,
nothing to admire ; there was everything in her life one would be thankful not to have in his.

Yet there was somewhat there one
did not see with the eyes. It was a
thing which received its name and is
most frequently mentioned by the un-
happy ; it was Happiness.

How had she with no earthly means
acquired it ?

The good God had come down from his throne and had given it to her. For He had found in her heart that by which He tempers his sovereignty over all worlds — compassion.

She, with no one to pity her, pitied every one in distress. For all such she knelt and prayed to God in secret. She knew that He was her friend and had been all her life and could not refuse her.

For whomsoever she heard of that was sick, afflicted, in misfortune, in shame, she went to God, as a mediator, for compassion. In her humble attic, the ante-chamber of Heaven, unknown to the sufferers themselves, she brought their woes and their burdens, their sins and their dangers, and made them known to the great Healer in nightly precatory vigils.

She was heard ; all that she asked was granted and thousands were healed, comforted, their sins covered. But they never knew how it happened. They thought it was the physician, or chance, or conscience ; or more often they never thought at all.

Forasmuch as she never remembered to ask anything for herself, the good God filled her heart with Happiness.

THE QUEEN'S HANDKERCHIEF

BORDERED with the finest Mechlin lace, which a fair Fleming wrought, bending over her cushion for three years, and with a centre of lawn tenuous as woven wind, the Queen, darling of all courts, having a hundred lovers at her feet, lifts the dainty fabric to her eyes and moistens it with six tears. The Queen, placed above mortal ills, on a throne that commands the universe, suffers and actually weeps.

It is a mystery ; no one knows why she suffers ; no one dares to comfort so great a personage ; and she continues to dampen with tears the centre of her handkerchief, careful not to spoil the border of such rare and costly Mechlin lace.

It would seem as if her Majesty had a heart, for she is still young and she weeps; and where else can tears come from save the heart? Cannot queens have all they wish for, and must they weep and suffer like other women?

But the Queen is lonely. Amid her hundred lovers she is solitary and has not one companion. They are puppets who surround her; respect, deference, reverence, the whole aulic pageant makes a desert about her. At other times she seems to herself on a mountain height, which no one may climb, and from which she cannot descend. At night it is even more dreary; for then she is ceremoniously disrobed and put to bed, and left to herself she weeps as if her heart would break, like a common distressed girl.

There is no doubt the Queen has a heart, but she has found that it is not her own. Such a discovery disconcerts even ordinary women. What can a queen do?

Is it any comfort to be able to wipe away tears with a beautiful Mechlin lace handkerchief, small and soft as a summer cloudlet?

The Queen has thought of something better to do with her handkerchief. She walks alone in her gardens. It is May and the earliest flowers are in blossom; not those flaming and profuse ones of June, but the white, the sensitive pale blue and faint pink, bearing upon frail stems delicate corollas that shut at a cloud and open at a sun-ray.

The Prince walks there too, grave, almost melancholy.

The Queen wanders toward him; her heart palpitates faster and faster as he approaches to salute her. She drops her handkerchief of Mechlin lace as she bends her sovereign eyes upon him. He stoops and offers it to her. She seems not to notice, to see; she will not take it, and she passes on to her ivy seat under the immemorial oak of her ancestors. She gathers, ere she seats herself, a bunch of violets and snowdrops which she pulls to pieces as the Prince follows and seats himself beside her.

Doubtless queens and princes make love, when they love, like others. Are there not smiles and silences and tears?

Doubtless only a prince could be so extravagant as to wipe away the happy tear-drops from the cheek of a queen with the very border of her Mechlin lace handkerchief. Even the Queen herself no longer cares what happens to it. It has had its day, its tears of pain and joy. But the Prince treasures it as a souvenir all his blessed life.

THE MASK VEIL

A DREAM STORY

IT is objected that the connections of incident and persons in dreams are often too grotesque and inconsequential to warrant any interpretation, either as recoveries of a past or shadowings of a future life. But this morning, awaking from a long dream and remembering it distinctly and considering it with particular care, I see no greater want of connection, at least, than in the conversation of four persons, of whom I was one, which soon after took place at the breakfast-table. For half an hour these four persons conversed, speaking now of this, now of that, and running on from one subject to another, with no obvious sequence. In truth, the glancing, unconscious associations to whose observation I chanced to have my mind drawn on that particular occasion, curiously resembled the occurrences of the dream from which I was fresh. What took place in my mind in dreaming was not more unreasonable and disconnected, in fact, very nearly represented the movements of the mental machinery of the other members of the sociable quartet at the breakfast-table.

Now I will tell my dream; but I forewarn the reader that it is not sensational, ghostly, prophetic, nor even farcical. It cost me some tears in the dreaming, which may have been those suppressed ones of the experience it seemed to adumbrate.

In the evening, before I slept, I had been listening to music, and had been myself singing in some part songs, taking, as was my custom, the baritone passages. Among the instrumental pieces that had been played was the popular score of the Carnival of Venice. It made no particular impression upon me, although no music goes unheard where I am. A hand organ stops me on the street, and a street band will delay me for quarter of an hour. It is true, walking on, I have a rather sheepish feeling, as if I had not held myself up to a standard of musical dignity, or had indulged a somewhat low taste.

As I have said, I had been singing as well as listening. Every one has his own especial habit or custom of doing certain things on retiring and rising. Some must have a nightcap jorum ; others eat ; others read themselves into repose before their hour of forgetfulness. I have a friend who loves at the end of the evening to talk of ghosts and immortality. This which seems to soothe him disturbs me. My friend, however, is the most restless of men, and nothing less than a ghost and the thought of eternity are adequate to bring him, even after

laborious days, into a state of repose
and moments of silence ; silence, which
generally frightens and perturbs him
as it does some children. As for myself, music enters me most sweetly into
the realm of sleep and dreams, and
the hopes and plans of the morrow.
Under its influence I feel more power-
fully every human attachment. I love
my friends better, and my life. I plan
noble deeds, and a perfected world
seems more possible. It flatters me
that all is well ; that there is some
power round about us greater than
ourselves, which softly disperses every
fear.

I sing merely to entertain myself
and my family, who are not severe
critics of the science of music, of
which I know nothing. For me it is
merely the expression of feeling ; when
it passes beyond, to complex ideas, I
cannot follow. Having used a good
many words in the course of my life,
and never finding them very faithful

pictures of the thing in my mind, it
is a boon to discover a vehicle that
expresses the inmost emotion — to
yourself if not to others.

Ah, that is sometimes the charm
of it, that you can pour forth the full
heart and never another is the wiser.
You can safely sing the secret which
you cannot speak. Music is Mercury's
invisible cloak; and it takes up and
carries on the movements of the soul
when language and thinking falter.

Having sung out of my heart an
otherwise inexpressible emotion, I
went to bed and fell into a deep sleep,
in which I dreamed that I was in
Venice. It was not Carnival time.
Still the sounds of the piece of music
I had just heard — the Carnival of Venice — were somehow present, and a
sort of accompaniment to all that tran-
spired. This was certainly curious, that
the mere name of a piece of music
should transport me to Venice and the
music itself all the while go sounding

on. Yet there I certainly was, in my
old quarters, the second floor of an
ancient, decayed palace on an unfre-
quented canal. The large room in
which I seemed to be sitting was
rather bare of furniture, and at that
instant two chairs only were visible,
one of which I occupied, the other a
lady, veiled. Soon another chair mys-
teriously appeared as a third person
entered the room.

But I have not explained who the
second person besides myself was, and
with whom I was talking. It was a
lady whom I had not seen for a very
long time, and whom I had no expectation, and little wish, of ever meeting
again. We had been formerly intimate ; and, as is often the case, I was
more fond of her than I suspected ;
she, alas ! less fond of me than she
appeared. So we parted.

She had not changed in looks ; but
her face, naturally very animated, had
grown calmer and a thought more pale.

Her veil, for she was in street costume, was drawn until it just covered her lips — a very translucent yet closely netted veil it was. I recognized it as the same I had sometimes dared to raise. It really hid nothing of feature or expression. But one dissembles easier behind howsoever thin a barrier.

We were conversing very earnestly as of old, yet quietly. Seized with a sudden impulse, I arose and leaning over her head was about to kiss her brow, as in our former intimacy she sometimes permitted. The veil suddenly changed to a mask of steel and hid her face, her brow. I started back in astonishment and terror, when, as quickly as the veil had been transformed, it now resumed its natural appearance.

"This is my punishment," said she, and tears began to fall upon her pallid cheek.

"I suffer the doom of an evil fate.

Do you not see that this veil has become the outward reality of the part I
played with you so lightly, so thought-
lessly?

"I have come in the hope that you
can release me from the spell — you
who once loved me so well. I — I
then had no heart; you were creating
it when you abandoned me in despair.
Oh, what have I suffered since that
time! My heart, like a seed long
in cold earth, at length lived, but the
more it grew into the light the bitterer
its pains and regrets. I have come" —
Her voice choked with tears.

Then I, though unable myself to speak
from surprise and emotion, still standing by her side, laid my hand upon her
head and endeavored to soothe and
calm her.

"I have come — I thought if you
would but even kiss me, this terrible,
mysterious veil would be destroyed.
But I see it cannot be — it is too
late!"

Her distress was too great for words ; and I was too much mystified to find any.

The music, which I had never ceased to hear, suddenly stopped. It seemed to me that if it would only go on I could in some way save my beautiful friend from her unaccountable destiny.

Quicker than I can write it the third person of the dream-drama, a lady, entered the room, and some invisible hand placed a chair from some invisible quarter. Before I had time to notice attentively what was going on the lady had seated herself, and I recognized in her another old acquaintance, but one with whom I had formerly maintained a relation exactly the reverse of that with my other friend. To tell the truth, I never could endure her. Alas ! it is my misfortune to be too amiable, and to deceive through my good heart the too enamored or too careless companion. So I have raised many a cup to my lips which I never cared to drink.

In spite of its being but the phantasm of a dream, the appearance of this lady had a natural and rational connection with its other events. For my intercourse with her was founded and followed up from the sympathy of our musical tastes. She was a famous amateur pianist, and always, when not seated at the piano, the most nervous, fidgety person in the world. It was with extreme difficulty she could enter a room and sit down in a chair; and one was seized with a thousand apprehensions as to what would happen before she became settled. Her long, beautiful hands were never still; they seemed to be forever playing over an invisible keyboard; and her lips and eyes moved and glanced in unison with the movements of her hands.

I know not how, but as soon as she entered I heard the music begin again; and it seemed to enter and proceed from her. She did not speak; some wonderful change had come over her too, for she sat motionless — not a finger of her hands moved. She was either herself listening to those almost spiritual strains of music, or was she producing them? The absence of the means of any effect is a small matter in dreams; indeed, we are never inquisitive after causes or instruments, and the fact of there being no piano or other instrument in the room never occurred to me as a reason why she should not be playing, or why the music should not be heard.

Did something more strictly spiritual connect itself with these occurrences? Was it that I had control of a power that did not need any material organ?

At any rate, I now saw present the lady whom I have just described, for the first time in my life, with real pleasure. She seemed to be an angel of love and deliverance, and to be in the power of my will, to be herself the instrument, rather than the player, and I its master.   For the music had returned with her; and it had, I know not how, been borne in upon me that my lovely friend, whose heart had returned to me after long separation and grief, could not be rescued from the fatal mask, which [worn as a veil to conceal herself, and behind which she was too fond of coquetry and dissembling] had become her prison, except by the power of music.

Once more, then, I bent over her beseeching face and loving eyes — in vain!   The mask grew solid again and glittered like the bosk of a shield, hiding all of her face to the chin.   I cast a troubled yet authoritative look at the silent witness of our hapless effort.

"Sing," she cried out, while her hands began to sweep over imaginary keys.   "I am not able by mere mechanical sounds to remove this dire-

ful Nemesis from your afflicted friend.
But add your voice to the accompaniment and the enchantment, the curse,
will be removed, yes, will be expiated."

Then I resumed the song I was
singing ere I fell asleep, in which her
image and the memory of my love had
mingled and thrilled me with powerful,
manifold emotions.

We can do two things at once in
dreams as easily as one ; and while I
sang in unison with the distant, wonderful accompaniment, I bent down,
this time to the lips of my beloved,
and our souls met and united like the
voice and the instrument, which all
the while kept sounding on. The
veil faded into a filmy cloudlet no
larger than a leaf and floated away.

The room became silent ; the player
and mediator had disappeared. My
companion arose ; she put her arms
around me and was beginning to
speak when my joy awoke me — to
find myself alone, forever alone !

WHAT is going on in the little red house that stands close to the road by Bellinghame to Milford town? Nothing, reader, unless you have been alive a long time without forgetting your very earliest memories; which, however fresh and dear to yourself, are of no consequence to another.

On this midsummer afternoon the little red one-storied house is vacant; the family have moved their chairs and crickets out to the shade of the orchard and are busily employed in braiding straw — braiding and chattering. Behold a group of women, a mother and her three daughters, almost grown, and her one small boy, whose dress and hair do not distinguish his sex. The turf is not fully knitted over the grave of the only man of the family. That

is why mother and children braid
straw, from breakfast to dinner, to
supper, and sometimes far into night.
The mother presides over the work ;
the eldest daughter prepares the
slender meals with such quickness
that she succeeds in braiding as many
yards a day as the others. Not a moment must be lost. The rent, that
most tragic of all human affairs, must,
must be paid at the end of every and
all months of all years. They are
cheerful, nevertheless ; they chatter
on, they even sing sometimes, but in
low, soft tones, such as best please the
mother, whose heart has not yet
healed. That delight of the church
chorister, the " Prime Flower of
Florid," she hates, if she could hate
anything. But you see by her low,
broad brow, her soft dark eyes, wide
apart, that she is all gentleness. One
of her daughters resembles her. The
other two are blue and blonde, and
the brother is of their type. There

are strange contrasts in the family, as if the hereditaments of five different ancestors had at length succeeded in asserting themselves in distinct form and character. For the present, however, they are united in a sympathetic bond. Affection unites them ; helplessness unites, and poverty, next to passion, most forceful binder of hearts and hands.

And so it is that with one feeling the ten hands of the brave and virtuous family braid the straw which gives them food, clothing and shelter, while the Father of the fatherless gives them happiness. Braiding straw only engages the fingers, and not quite so much as knitting ; the head and tongue and other bodily parts are free to entertain themselves as they please. One can even walk and continue the occupation, and read a book, as if doing nothing else. I can braid a little ; my stint is one yard a day. When I am one year older it will be two, then three, and so on, an added yard for each year, until I am too old for such feminine employment and am dismissed from the company of women, or perhaps aroused from it by the sight of a gun or a plough, as the young Achilles hidden among women by a sword.

The family sits braiding, and it is a good time to look at the little red house, and ever and anon the eyes of one or another are lifted and turn toward it with fondness. I myself, who am but a child boy, the youngest of the circle, realize what the house contains much more vividly when out of it than when in it. Although we call it the red house, we mean that it was once red, some blotches of which remain on its sides, abraded by the suns and storms of a hundred seasons. But this does not affect me; I do not even see the walls; I am looking through them. I see every room and the furniture of each. I see

the kitchen; its fireplace, its two small
windows, its five high-backed, rush-
bottomed chairs; its round table, with
a short stem and three branching legs,
through which I am still small
enough to crawl, on every day but
Sunday, when it is turned up and set
against the wall. Then it always
seems to me to be going to meeting,
because, like myself, it is washed and
scrubbed on Saturday night and looks
very white and different. As yet I
do not like the Puritan Sabbath — as
much as I shall when I grow up to
become clerk of the parish. It is one
day in coming and another in going. I
am already so sensitive to what others
feel that I feel without knowing why.
I become with them serious, secretly
miserable, from which I scarcely re-
cover before Tuesday.

Ah, now I look at the little red
house with joy, while my fingers weave
over and under the long, narrow
straws, the motion of whose extreme

ends resembles the waving antennæ
of some great insect, some saurian ant
or bee. The room I least often enter
I see with the greatest distinctness.
It is the parlor; it is our pride, our
sole remaining evidence of better days,
of respectable, rustic gentility. The
sheriff did not take it! It is where
I walk softly and feel subdued. I cannot hear my footsteps, and it almost
frightens me to feel something soft
under my feet. I look down and the
stripes and colors of the carpet seem
too good to walk upon. There are six
chairs, arranged in pairs, turned a little toward each other, as if ready for
conversation, almost vocal with those
common greetings — " How have you
been ? " " Will you lay aside your
things ? " " I am so glad to see you ! "
These much prized chairs are always
in the same place; they themselves
would protest against any change; the
whole family would resent it. Every
day one of the daughters goes in to

see that they are in their rightful
places. She murmurs as she goes,
"Some one may come." They have
gilt figures on the backs and on the
two side spindles. I rest my elbows
on the seats and look up and wonder
at those resplendent figures. A sense
of something greater than myself
comes over me. It is the first step.
It is only some crude, gilded tracery,
resembling thin bands of clouds, spi-
raled and wreathed by the wind. As
I do not know what it means, it is
greater than I. In the corner is an
open wood stove ; it has brass knobs
on its flat top and brass cylinders sunk
in its iron jambs. On either side the
stove are the brass-handled shovel and
tongs in their ear-shaped rests, on one
of which hangs the bellows ; its convex
side is bright with Chinese figures in
blue and yellow. I never tire of blowing it, and then by way of reprisal,
blowing my breath back into its noz-
zle. But what I see with the fondest

pride, as I look toward the end of the little red house where the parlor is situated, are two pictures on the parlor wall. They are my own ; they are the only things in the world that I am conscious of possessing ; and they are in a place of honor — they are in our parlor ! They are the only things in the house with which I do not wish to play. I stand and look up at them absorbed, trying to think something ; and one of them looks at me, but the other does not. The former is the more precious ; it is a picture of two puppies with large, round eyes looking directly into mine. I believe they are real dogs because I can see on the other side of them. I have a longing to put my hands upon them, but they are too high up, and I begin to have a very curious feeling about things I cannot touch nor taste, and that have no other dimension than surface, as of something mysterious and dangerous. I revenge myself

on discovering the flat surface of the
pictures in my books by defacing
them. With a pin I prick out the
eyes of the whole " Browne Family "
in my little story-book when I find
that there is nothing on the other
side of the leaf. But as yet I believe
my dogs to be solid. I am already a
stern realist. Earth and water are
the only substances which completely
gratify me. There is enough of both,
and rarely do I have enough of anything I love.

Although I take equal satisfaction
in being the owner of the other picture,
it does not make so much impression
upon me. It is a picture of two children, a boy and girl, in blue and white
dresses. Both have fair hair falling
in curls over their shoulders. On the
boy's hand is perched a dove, and his
eyes are turned upon it ; but those of
his companion are fixed upon him.
If she would only look away sometimes, would look at me, I should like

her better. Her steady gaze upon that boy puzzles me. I conclude after much reflection that he is her brother.

There is only one other thing that draws my attention from my work; it is the river, the placid Charles, my plaything summer and winter; yonder it slides under the stone arch, and on through a mile of alders bent over with the weight of wild grapevines, making an aerial, verdant bridge all the way. In vain do I imagine where the stream can be going. I have been told many times that it flows into the ocean. Ocean? What is it? No one knows; no one has seen it. Nevertheless I know where the river begins, and I follow it up to where it is so narrow that with a run and a great spring I can jump across. "What, can you jump across the Charles River?" This will be questioned me when I reach its mouth and find what great things are boasted there. And I shall answer with pleasant irony: "But you see I began very young to leap your wide Boston Charles ; it also was young.''

At length my yard, my stint, is done. I lay it in my mother's lap, who praises its evenness, kisses me, and tells me that I may now go and play. Then I run to a certain tree under which I keep my wheels, my boxes, my strings, my nails, and I forget the little red house and all that concerns it. I am now in my own kingdom, in the midst of my own affairs, where I create and destroy worlds with all the magic machinery of an arch thaumaturgist.

THE recluse of Valencita, in whose bosom the light of love had been extinguished for several weeks, sat before his darkening hearth holding a small portfolio now empty and flat. A spark reillumined for a moment the red jambs and sooty back of the fireplace; it slowly ignited the sacrifice about to be offered up in memory and obliteration of a star that came across the whole expanse of the heavens and stood for many nights above his hermitage.

There were only four letters; but three were thick, thick almost as an Aldine classic, and contained many closely written sheets; not a space was left; postscript followed postscript, round and round the margins, across and across like a triple palimpsest,

until at last no room was remaining
for the final words which seemed to
hesitate, to linger, to refuse themselves to the pen.

The fourth, which was the first in
date, was thinner, in more careful
penmanship and more timid of words ;
much fair paper was unblotted, and it
ended half way down the last page, but
ended with a word, a sigh, a something
that kindled into love as the embers
upon the hearth now kindled its corpse.

The letters burned slowly; they
were compacted and saturated with
close lines of ebon ink ; this and the
obduracy of loving words, were they
not resisting the fiery extinction ? At
length the edges blazed ; the heat
opened the pages ; they began to roll
up, and a faint crepitating protest
arose, quite to the heart of the
watcher. Soon every leaf separated
itself from every other, as if each one
would now try to save itself only, like
the scorched victims of a conflagration.

Then the flames swept them only the more furiously. More and more madly they ran in and out among the helpless leaves, chasing each other back and forth like frenzied, avenging spirits. A few stood out defiantly —the true inconsumable sentences !

On the blackened sheets, now reduced to an izzle, could be discerned some still blacker lines of ink; yes, even words, from which had fallen away all grosser material, as the tissue falls from the leaf leaving but tracery ; and looking down into the immolated heap the recluse read with perfect distinctness — " I am still thine."

THE DEVIL'S BARGAIN

THE Devil diffuses himself with enormous strides and short calls when he alights on the shores of New Hampshire. The air is too heavy for flying and he is compelled thus to walk. The shore of New Hampshire is only a day's journey; but for him he passes over it like the wind which continually blows there. And like the wind he enters the wide-mouthed chimneys and greets those who are expecting him.

To-night the little store-keeper expects him. He is counting ninepences, on each one of which he has made half a cent in his day's bartering. When he sells anything he calls the silver piece worth twelve cents; when he buys, thirteen. Thus has he become the richest of all his neighbors. The Devil chuckles as he sees him at this business and grows fonder of him. He desires his soul and has offered a handsome bargain for it, whereby there is to be a shorter road to wealth than the ninepenny one for the little store-keeper.

The Devil steps softly and peers in upon him. He delights to witness his employment.

"Aha! little man, there is no longer need to count so carefully thy base silver. Gold! Dost thou not know the look of it? It gleams like the sun! Away with that pale, ignoble stuff, only fit for the palms of slaves and beggars! Thou shalt have gold, bright gold! more than flashed on Solomon's Temple or irisated the corridors of Cæsar's palace."

The little store-keeper stood up; his eyes dilated with expectation. His silver seemed dross; his riches ineffable poverty.

"When, when shall I see the good gold?" he cried.

"To-night! ere the cock crows, or ever the sun makes the sign of the golden eagle on the horizon! Hang thou thy largest and longest legged boot in the chimney corner, and I will pour down from above more than shall fill it of such gold as thou never hast seen, even in dreams over thy clipped and greasy silver."

The little store-keeper was in ecstasies, for he bethought him of the boots with the long legs, so long he never could wear them.

"To-night, I say, ere the cock crows, or ever the sun makes the sign of the golden eagle on the horizon — hearest thou? And thy soul when thou hast done with it, it shall be mine. Art thou agreed?"

The store-keeper thought twice; he was sharp witted. A little more and a little less were always in his mind when he bargained.

"Beshrew thy hard bargain," said he. "Thou mayest fill it twice as well as once, what difference to thee, and then I shall be thine after the gold has comforted me through my life."

" Thou rogue! I see thou hast an eye for the ruddy gold despite thy up-gathered and unprofitable silver. A mountain of it shall be as dust under thy feet."

The little trader's heart expanded, and his little eye twinkled like a steely star in the remotest heavens. He loved a sharp bargain and few words to the making of it. Never had he compassed one so much after the manner of his liking.

"Gold! thou shalt have enough of it! One night shall fill all thy bags and chests ; for that thy soul! The second night thy cellar and thy well shall hardly contain it. But beware, thou rogue, that thou dost not forfeit the days of thine earthly life, seeing they were well enough spent with thy silver and thy sly trafficking.

" Remember! ere the cock crows, or

ever the sun makes the sign of the
golden eagle on the horizon ! And if
I come a second time, listen for the
roaring of the wind in thy chimney and
the rote of the sea on thy shore where
a hundred wrecks lie rotting ! "

At night he remembered his word
and filled the boot-leg of the smart
trader until it overran and half filled
the fireplace.

The second night the wind roared
in the great chimney. The rote of
the sea shrieked among the bones
of a hundred buried wrecks, and with
a great stride, his monstrous cloak
bellying in the wind, the Devil alighted
at the top of the chimney.

The little cheater was expecting
him. Sharper than the stiletto of a
Venetian assassin was his wit, and he
bethought him to cozen the Devil with
a trick surpassing all the rogueries of
Christendom ; yes, even those of that
paragon of all rogues, Hal Tufts, of
Lubberland in Durham town.

He hung his long-legged boot in the fireplace, but first he cut clean off the bottom !

The gold rattled down ; it poured through the leg of the boot ; it rolled and glittered and covered the floor and filled the room.

And still the Devil poured.

" Aha ! " said he at last. " Is it you, my little man ? Are you there ? I thought so. So — I am here — not for the last time neither, by my soul ! Ho there ! Now thou art mine, body — and soul, if thou hast one — in this life, and *down there !* Dost thou hear ?

" A cheap bargain ! But what trouble these mortals take to sell themselves, they who are already mine."

The Devil disappeared, but not far off was he.

The little trader now made haste to store his treasure into bags, barrels, chests and closets. The bags rent, the hoops flew from the barrels, the chests fell apart, the closet floor dropped out.

"There is the cellar and the well," thought he.

No sooner was the gold packed into the cellar than the bottom sank out of sight, and as it disappeared he heard the Devil laugh.

"The well will hold the remainder," he moaned, "and the water will hide it."

The water received it with a gurgle that sounded like the laughter of fiends. Then all vanished. The bottom fell out of the well — the bottom fell out of everything!

With a groan the poor trader returned to his counter, his scales, his yardstick and his ninepences.

"Silver is good enough for me," he said. Still no bottom would stay in anything. Jugs, canisters, casks, even his money drawers and his breeches pocket became merely tunnels through which all their various contents streamed out and went to waste.

"Oh, that accursed boot-leg!" he groaned.

His spirit was broken ; his mind went out ; his body withered away.

He died and was buried. Such a burial ! Oh, the horror of the mourners to see when his coffin was lowered — to see the bottom fall out of the grave and the coffin disappear ! And an infernal laugh went up from the black and yawning pit through which it sank ; then a mocking voice — " Aha ! Are you here, my little trader, my sweet ninepence, my thrifty boot-leg ? "

THE SOUL OF THINGS

My father bequeathed to me the whole of his estate and the friendship of his ancient neighbors and companions. He communicated to me, from time to time, his experience, accumulated in a long life of action and suffering, and I was betimes instructed in all the wisdom of the elder sages and poets by their most celebrated successors. I looked about the world ; I saw nothing more to be desired.

I sat down among my possessions, contemplating them in grateful tranquillity, thankful neither to have purchased nor earned any of them. For I lived in an age and among a people whose activities were altogether commercial. If I deserved my possessions, it was not on account of my own efforts or merits, but those of my father

and a long line of fortunate ancestors.

Unambitious and easily satisfied, I
readily discovered my lot in life which,
like that of Ulysses, I found thrown
contemptuously aside and long neg-
lected. From the first, and before I
became conscious of any choice, I enjoyed nothing so much as sitting still
and meditating on the soul of things.
This vague phrase pleased me more
than the exact language of science, or
that of the masters of other sorts of
learning. This was in my youth. It
seemed to me that with leisure, in
silence and with a free mind, I might
come nearer to knowing the material
world and interpreting its life, its soul,
than by experiment and analysis.

When I speak in the active voice,
as if I could come nearer, it is a figure
of speech, similar to that which we
use when we speak of the sun's rising and setting. It was I that was to
remain fixed ; it was things which were

to come nearer, which were to rise and
reveal themselves. I confess that all
I know of nature, of things, and of all
animals save man, of whom I know
little but by tradition, I have learned
by sitting still, looking on or listening. Everything comes more than half
way toward the man who is still. The
bird alights upon his head as upon a
bough.

Thus have I often become aware of
the soul of things, and that inanimate
as they seem and are declared to be,
they all have a faculty of expression.
Yes, I have seen the leaves move
without wind ; I have seen trees bend
and grow toward each other, and one
hand of the Traveler's Joy clasp the
fingers of another. I have seen water
lilies on their long, flexile footstalks,
though anchored deep in mud, draw
closer. Who has not seen drops of
water run together? and who was
ever satisfied to call it capillary attrac-
tion ? I have seen the next flower

open at the edge of the bank where
the first had opened, and all again
close in due reverse order. I need not
speak of the notes of birds and insects
which have but one fixed meaning,
clear, simple and certain ; nor the hum
of bees about their queen, the waving
antennæ of ants on meeting ; nor musical notes which make the dust of the
earth assume the forms of stars and
shells and flowers, by an ascending
tone adding a new petal until the co-
rolla is complete, and by a full octave
arranging particles of matter in circles
and globes. Nor have I a doubt that
the fragrance of some flowers is their
soul, and that it resembles what we
call character in people, a subtle thing
that goes forth without action or effort.

But why should I accumulate and
enumerate examples like a school-
book ; for there is never any possibil-
ity of completing the list ; and words
do not signify nor translate the meth-

ods of expression common to the soul
of things. They are inexpressible and
invisible ; but the invisible is all that
is worth seeing, the inexpressible all
that is worth listening to.

I SAT down by the door; by the door of my house I sat down and wept.

" Door," said I, " have you closed at last upon all that was lovely, all that I loved ? "

Here we came in youth ; the door opened widely ; lightly in trooped all the joys and the hopes ; the earth smiled ; the sea sang a thousand different songs ; the days were long.

Children were born, and we were glad.

The rose died ; the stripling oak was uprooted.

Love divided grief, and we lived on.

In the spring, in the little field, a violet bloomed ; and in the summer, by the porch, an eglantine.

All tears were wiped away. The door still opened as wide as ever. But the prospect narrowed, became more distant, more indistinct, and the waves of the sea thundered on the outer reefs.

The days grew shorter. There were signs and omens ; we turned our eyes away ; but they also turned and faced us.

Then the long, dark procession, speechless, veiled, passed over the threshold, never returning.

And I myself closed the entrance, always so unsuspectingly open ; and I said, now shall I keep the remnant that is left ; and I thrice bolted and barred that deceiving and voracious door.

It was in vain ! in vain !

The living now escaped from it, I knew not how, and I alone was left within.

Beautiful ghosts were my companions. Often too I saw one from which the limbs had been torn ; bleeding from its eternal wounds that healed but to reopen, it looked down upon me with remediless agony. It was myself ; unable any longer to bear the sight, I fled through the door. Of it-self it closed behind me, and I heard for the last time the bolts rattle in their sockets.

And I sat down by the door and wept.

THE VOICE

GABRIEL could hardly keep his eye-
lids from closing on the book he was
reading, pages which reflected a new
dreamer's dream. He too was a
dreamer. But an irresistible languor
continually overcame him, in which he
seemed to be carried far away among
strange and weeping faces. It was
not that he was more weary than usual
or more sad. He had finished his
day's vain and impossible task, with
bent brow and impetuous pen. Now
at ease in the disengaged hour, he resigned the possession of himself to
the new writer. Slowly he lost him ;
his head sank, his eyes closed. Yet
he was wide awake ; his mind did not
sleep ; it was traversing an immense
space in intense pursuit of something.

Suddenly some one called, "Gabriel!" He put his feet from the chair and leaned forward. The voice called again "Gabriel! Gabriel!" It seemed to come from the door; he arose joyfully, for he knew the voice, and opened, but no one was there. He stepped across the threshold; twilight was there and silence. "Ah, she is amusing me; she wishes to surprise me. She has come; that voice could be no other's; there is none like it in the world!" "Gabrielle!" he called, "where are you? Do not tantalize me."

He stood a long time at the open door. Then he reëntered his room. "She must be here," he murmured. But all the chairs were empty and the room was stiller than before. He went to the window; again he went to the door; he knew she must be near; the voice was hers. He recognized it more surely now than at first, for it kept on sounding in his ears. It called aloud no more. Still he knew she must be near, and he waited for her to spring suddenly from her hiding, from her little pleasantry, into his arms. Long he listened; long he waited. Often he went to door and window. Day grew into darkness; the night reigned and divided her realm among a thousand stars. Gabriel sat long, immovable, expectant, so that his heart beat harder and harder. He was more awake than he had been in all his life. The voice became to him certain and real; the mystery more impenetrable. Just when he thought he should watch the night out, and even felt he could never again close his eyes, he fell asleep. So soundly he slept! He heard no voice, he dreamed no dream. In the morning he awoke and it seemed to him that he had been dreaming a long time, or rather listening to the voice of a dream. "It is nothing," said he; "let us to work." "It is nothing," said he;

" the words of the book I was reading
came to life, they spoke ; but why
should they call, 'Gabriel'?"

He thought no more about it ; he resumed his task, as everything does in
the morning. The tide of the laborious, ineffectual sea flowed by his window; the new sun streamed through
it ; the grass lightly waved a longer
streamer ; the trees trembled as their
roots shot deeper into the earth. A
faint humming arose over the whole
sad, toiling world. In it one might
hear the murmur of a myriad tongues,
hearts, brains, hands, feet, all eagerly
demanding of the day bread, fame, gold,
love, increase of joy or surcease of pain.
Gabriel's pen joined in the chorus.
He wrote everything and failed in all.
Fame followed him not. No one heard
him. He wrote, he read the sentence,
the page aloud to himself. What was
the matter with it? Then he wrote
poetry, finished, tenuous, unassailable,
panoplied with every grace and art,

finest grains of gold dipped from the streams whose founts were in mythic lands, poetry, almost poetry. He bent his brow, he worked harder than ever; not for gold, not for fame, but with an insatiable passion to pour out upon the page all that he knew, all that he observed, all that he felt.

Did he know, had he observed, had he ever felt? Yes; but as the leaf folded in the bud, before it has been rained upon, smitten by whirlwinds, shriveled by the sun, pierced by frost, and at length blown into the mud and trampled by the implacable, Rhadamanthine feet of men and women. All these things he could paint with a dainty hand, not as having suffered himself, but distantly, as the ancient tautologies of human destiny. So the bud safely folded, fold on fold, softly chanted of the leaf and what was about to happen to it, knowing as much as youth knows of age, as much as the inquisitor knows of the martyr.

So the bud, safely folded, fold on fold, softly chanted of the unfolded leaf.

That day Gabriel arose from his table and his papers and a voice within cried, " It is futile ; this is neither red with redness, nor black with blackness. Thou callest it now red, now black, and commandest thy readers to observe as much. But life, life itself is not there ! "

Then Gabriel said, " I will journey ; perhaps I shall come back with a wiser mind."

" I will go to her whom I love. I will bring her home with me ; and life shall teach me. Through her I shall know all."

For three days and nights he hastened on, and he arrived at her door as the night fell. He entered joyously ; high his heart beat and already he felt the embrace of Gabrielle.

The rooms were silent ; the draperies were unlooped ; the ebony furniture shone with a metallic lustre, like the caskets of the dead. Women, clothed in black, sat in the shadowed recesses, weeping. He stopped ; a terror seized him. "Where is she?" said Gabriel.

"She called for thee," said one ; "thou didst not come and she departed without thee. She said, these were her last words, that she should go to thee and never be separated again. Hast thou not seen her?"

"No ;" said Gabriel. "But I heard her call, and I have looked everywhere for her ; it was her voice then ! Ah, I knew it must be."

"Yes," said one. "When Death had even himself called to her, she arose, and with a wandering mind went from room to room, imploring thy name, Gabriel, in such a tone thou wouldst have heard though thyself dead. Then she slept a little space, she slept, and awoke happy, for she said she had seen thee reading in a book and afterward the door opened for her. Then her eyes closed and did not look again ; she breathed and there was yet a smile at the corners of her mouth, and we could not tell when she ceased to be. We know only she has gone from us to thee. Thou must return speedily, for she is already there and awaiting thee."

For three days and nights Gabriel traveled back, but his spirit went on before, and he did not note either the night or the day. It was autumn ; the leaves were falling, and in the north the weltering sea grew green under the horizontal sun.

Gabriel reëntered his room. Nothing was changed but himself. He listened again for the voice and heard it now in his bosom. He listened more and more for the voice ; the tears fell upon the page and formed themselves into words, sentences, strophes. For a long time yet no one else heard the voice ; or, if they chanced to hear, stayed only to mock, or to assure themselves that it was no voice at all, the mere passing, spring piping of the hylas in the roadside ditch.

At length it changed; now it seemed to listeners to come from the trees, and now, wonderful! from the highest pinnacle of the mountain. And some affirmed it came from heaven itself.

THE WRITER'S WALK

HAVING finished his morning's allotted task, the writer of beautiful books bethought him to walk awhile and cool his flagrant brain.

As usual, he set forward in the direction of peaceful seclusion, where he could at once calm himself and conduct his plots and portray his characters for the next day's fixation upon the precious pages.

Delightful labor! to create as it were out of nothing, yes, out of one's own head, scenes, dialogue, even persons that would seem to every one real, verisimilar, though the readers should never have known or seen the like; to cause them to think they had, what so wonderful illusion in the world! And there is no good author who does not flatter his readers after this manner.

No wonder the writer of beautiful books turned away from crowded streets and the habitations of men whose walls touch in order more securely to separate them. Not there could he find the stuff that he needed for the creative alembic.

But of a sudden, he knew not how, an impulse came over him to turn short about and walk among the streets, among men and women. Then, as is usual to the reflective mind, he considered his impulse and how he should make it profitable. And as one seldom can divest himself entirely of the business he is about, he said to himself, "I will see what I can find among actual men and women to identify and verify these pictorial beings I am now clothing with faculties, ideas and personality." Finally, as merely looking gave him but little satisfaction, it occurred to him to salute some of the people he met with and engage their attention long enough to discover if they were at all like his inventions.

"Good-morrow," said he, to a man who was mixing mortar for a new block of houses already built to the third story.

"Good-morrow to yourself," answered the mixer of mortar.

"How smoothly the mortar runs off your hoe," said the writer of beautiful books.

"Yes, indeed; after you have pulled it through a thousand times and get it tempered right, then it sticks to nothing but the bricks. The hoe leaves a wake behind it like a steamboat; and the mortar comes off the hoe like the wave from the rock."

"Good-day," said the writer of beautiful books.

There now, thought he to himself, that is the way it should be with my sentences; they should adhere only to the characters for whom they are tempered. And the man knows a si-

militude when he sees it. In fact, he
knows his own business pretty well.

But then, he did not have to create
his lime and sand. 'T is easy to mix
when you have the ingredients.

Then he walked on, and stopped
where a number of others were standing, mostly ladies, in front of a great
show-window. A profusion of silks,
velvets, and laces hung from the ceiling to the floor, falling in rich dark
folds, or soft, negligent trails, so that
one instinctively thought, what splendid costumes they would make for
one's wife or sister ! As if in response
to this secret feeling, figures came
forth in the same or equally gorgeous
panoplies and faultless fittings, circling
slowly and monotonously in never-ending minuet on their hypothetic feet,
displaying every possible attribute of
the materials and the style. You would
have thought yourself at one of Ma-
dame Pompossiter's receptions. It was
quite irresistible.

Then as if to turn the window of stuffs and dummies to some account, the writer of beautiful books soliloquized whether, on the whole, it were not easier to dress up a dummy in perfectly good English, choice, apposite English, than an actual English being; whether such language, especially in conversational passages, was not more important than anything else to promote the illusion of reality. He was almost persuaded.

But he had come into a crowded street where he was liable to be noticed if he saluted anybody, and his quest did not seem at all accomplished. So he turned into a less frequented thoroughfare.

He came anon to a beggar, who appeared to have nothing to do but sit at her receipt of customs. He stopped and gave her an unusual alms. Her blessing was correspondingly large and emphatic. He talked with her a little while, and found her diction singularly fitted to her occupation. She spoke in the idiom of experienced beggars; it was not wanting in finesse and picturesqueness. It was not often she had a chance to talk with a passer-by.

The writer of beautiful books was impressed by it, and remembered some of her epithets and adjectives. But she herself did not answer his purpose. He had never created anything of that kind; nor yet mortar-mixers. As to the dummies in the show-window they came nearer to his notion, as they left so much room for contrivance and embellishment. And he walked on, speaking with various people, learning many new things, observing various characteristics in speech, manners, and mind among his fellow-beings. But none seemed to answer exactly his purpose; none were comparable to those that had grown up in his imagination in the stillness and solitude of his study.

Then he turned back homeward, and resuming his pen, the writer of beautiful books exclaimed, as if he had suddenly solved the riddle of the Sphinx, " If we must create, let us do as the gods ; let us create out of nothing ! "

THE SECRET OF AUTHORSHIP

ALTHOUGH always known, the secret of authorship has never before been divulged.

We were talking of its pains and pleasures, my friend and I, and how we happened to become writers. " I do not wonder," I was saying, " so much how I began to write as why I continue."

" Do you recall," said he, " when you did begin ? "

" No," I replied, " I do not, except in the vaguest way."

" Well, then," said he, " that is the difficulty with you ; that explains why you do not get on better with publishers and readers."

" Explain yourself," I exclaimed.

He complied, and went on to give an account of his own experience in beginning to write, which he pretended was the secret of his success and my want of it. Successful I knew he was; but why, had been to me somewhat inexplicable. Much as I esteemed him as a friend, and a companion from boyhood, I never found in the man himself a trace of that fine energy and those remarkable thoughts which appeared so profusely upon his pages. This seeming paradox was in some measure reconciled by the narrative which he proceeded to relate.

"You remember the old schoolhouse where you began your education about the time I had completed mine. Can you not still see its three tiers of benches and slanting desks on either side, rising one above another? The highest left not much room between the head of a tall boy like me and the ceiling. I was already advanced to this upper row of seats, that is, I was of an age to belong to the first, or highest class in the school. There were

four boys in the class and six girls.
Originally there had been the same
number, six, of each sex; but two
boys had dropped off, one to become a
clerk, the other a carpenter. We
thought we knew a great deal. It
was the age of extreme, self-conscious
wisdom. We were on very friendly
terms with our young and pretty
school-mistress. She treated us almost as equals; and we, on our part,
treated the lower classes of younger
children with almost contempt. We
could now read in the highest grade
reading-book, perform most of the examples at the end of the arithmetic,
and spell those bizarre and crucial
words which are never used or heard
of out of spelling-books. And, in
short, we were about to be graduated,
and were looked upon with awe by the
other scholars and with some pride by
our teacher, who allowed us certain
privileges on account of our age and
the dignity of an upper class. One of

the most prized of these privileges was that on warm summer afternoons, when the schoolhouse became uncomfortable and the small children restless and noisy, we were permitted to go out under the trees not far away and study and rehearse to each other our lessons for the next day. We were old enough to be safely intrusted with that liberty.

"In these little retreats from the school-room we usually separated into companionable couples who studied out of one book. It was singular how frequently it happened that there were only half as many books as scholars. Consequently it was necessary for each pair to sit close together to get their heads over the same page. It is true there were not quite enough boys to make up these fond couples; but there are always, fortunately, girls who much prefer each other to any boys whatever. In this way innocent attachments were formed, often lasting, oftener transient.

" The time came when we were to
write compositions, a new and untried
intellectual exercise, but considered
the last fine flower of our training.
Our school-mistress was much per-
plexed to find suitable subjects for all
of us, and when she had named eight
her resources were quite exhausted.
A happy thought came to her; she
would let two of us, a girl and boy,
choose our own topics. The lot fell
upon me and the girl I most affected.
We asked to be allowed to write our
compositions in our favorite academe
under the trees.   Our request was
granted.   So armed each one with
slate and pencil we went out, and each
pair chose its own little ambush where
to invite all the rustic muses to its
aid.

" My companion and I sought the
largest tree we could find, within
whose instepped bole we could sit and
find support. Here we sat down and
prepared to write. It was a dubious

situation ; no subject, and not an idea
in one's head. There was a profound,
distressing silence. I was waiting to
hear the sound of my companion's
pencil on her slate, for I thought her
beginning would insure mine. I did
not dare look at her. I experienced
more constraint than ever before, and
I was conscious that my credit was at
stake with her in this first momentous
effort. I felt something soft rustling
against me; and presently an arm
leaned over my shoulder. I looked up,
and met a pair of eyes fixed upon my
blank slate.

" 'Begin,' said she ; 'you must write
your own composition first, then for
me — will you not? I have heard that
those who love could — could inspire
— that was the word — each other. I
will look over, and when you make a
mistake, or hesitate, I will do that —
inspire, help you ; can I ? '

"I looked up into her trusting, expectant eyes, and I began. Yes, it

was then I began to write. Do you remember how much the teacher and friends praised the little essay, after it was copied out upon sheets of gilt-edged paper and tied with a ribbon for exhibition on our graduation day — tied and arranged, and in truth as good as written by that girl who is now my wife?

" So now my axiom is : no man can write well unless a woman looks over his shoulder ; and you see, old friend, why it is you don't succeed."

THE POOL

A SOCIALISTIC APOLOGUE

Two immense rivers flowed beside the greatest, the most magnificent city in the world. It was full of palaces filled with jewels, services of china and gold, a single piece of which was a fortune ; statues, pictures, and books, priceless, incomparable masterpieces, crowded the walls. Temples and theatres rose above even the proudest of the palaces, on which untold wealth had been lavished, and in which the most beautiful women and the most accomplished men alternately worshiped and amused themselves. All that gold could command for luxury, for display, for refinement, for patronage of all arts and sciences that make life ornamental or commodious was poured out in an abundant and ever increasing stream. All accidents or misfortunes that happened to other parts of the world, wars, famines, floods, failures of merchants or capital, the men of this city were able to take advantage of and make redound to the repletion of their already bursting coffers.

The prosperous cities around this metropolis, when they were most prosperous, sent their superfluous wealth, their ablest men and fairest women, to surcharge its dazzling streets, salons, palaces and temples. When not prosperous they went as supplicants to the proud emporium and brought back good fortune at fabulous, ruinous rates.

The two great rivers washed either side of the city, bringing down all the commodities of inland countries; and their commerce paid tribute both when it entered the city and when it returned from the seas beyond. Besides this the two rivers and the ocean at their mouth brought health to the citizens and the most delicious climate of the five zones.

But in the midst of the city was a Pool, not very large, but which was fed by a far-off stream — and generally invisible — that poured along a continuous current of noisome and pestilential waters. No drought seemed to affect it, nor yet rains; nor any season of the year. Frost froze it not; the suns of summer did not evaporate it. Only in the night, and on some sacred and secular holidays, and when the suffragists were preparing for their annual or quadrennial contests, did its volume seem to increase at all.

At times a deadly vapor arose from the Pool, destroying all who breathed it, alike the rich and the poor. The Pool was believed to be bottomless — and it was. And the far-off stream never ceased to flow and to fill it to the brim.

The city arose with all its mighty

energy, its colossal resources, to suppress the dreadful plague. The authorities attacked it on all sides with every known device and newest invented engines for pumping and sewerage ; innumerable conduits pierced its entire circumference. In vain ! not an inch could they lower the deadly abyss. The citizens volunteered, and with uninterrupted relays of buckets and private sluices endeavored to empty the foul pit of waters. Even ladies of the wealthiest and most luxurious families, doffing their more costly dresses and jewels, went down to the edge of the Pool, and with gloved hands and silver dippers essayed to alleviate the evil of which they had heard, but which as yet had hardly touched the hem of their garments. It even became fashionable to devote some afternoons to bailing at the troublesome spring. It became as it were an act of devotion ; a vicarious expiation for all their own blessings.

The ministers and devotees of the temples prayed and preached incessantly, and bade their worshipers to spare no effort or sacrifice to abate, or at least moderate, the scourge; to spend their wealth freely in the cause; and they declared as with one voice that thus only could the great opportunities and privileges of fortune and station be sanctified and the Pool become a means of redemption from too much worldliness.

At length, as all these efforts seemed in vain, and as no one had the hardihood to explore and attack the sources of the corrupt and maleficent Pool, since the stream in its long course turned millions of mills and was, though not openly admitted, the secret source of many of the greatest fortunes in the city, all classes of the more prosperous citizens, led by the priests and professional philanthropists, turned their attention to the founding and maintenance of every sort of charitable institution for the relief and care of those who had most directly suffered by the poison of the Pool. For when it did not at once kill those who breathed its vapors or who happened to fall into its waters, it had the singular effect of transforming its victims into sots, paupers, murderers, thieves, idiots, courtesans and beggars.

Then all the people rejoiced at the work of their benevolent hands, and they became proud of their hospitals, asylums and prisons, and vaunted them as the tokens of the highest civilization, the crown of the most sublime religion. The duty of the rich was taught and expounded even by millionaires themselves. And it now became plain, the unexpressed creed of the people, why some were unfortunate enough to have been contaminated or destroyed by the affliction of the Pool. It was that the spirit of charity might find exercise in the bosoms of the for-

tunate and the saved. In short, it was
a Providential Pool — a blessing in disguise ; and its reflex influence almost
more than compensated its monstrous
brood of ills.

Only a few differed from this view
and execrated it, and endeavored at
the peril of their lives to reach and to
redeem the upper waters of the insidi-
ous river. But they were such as had
no standing in society. They were
dreaded in all the temples and public
rostrums ; they were denounced by
the wealthy and sneered at by the
most astute political economists. The
evil has always existed and must always exist. It was inherent in the
constitution of the universe, handed
down by all the generations of our
forefathers, and the inevitable con-
comitant of vast cities and crowded
populations, they said. What age, what
city, had not its Pool? All we can do
is to mitigate the miseries of our own
— decently bury those whom it has

robbed of life, succor those whom it has infected. Let us apply our energies, our laws, our religion to the effects, not to the sources, of this black blot. The sources are beyond our jurisdiction ; the stream, well, that has too many interests attached to make its diversion or purification possible.

Still the few, the few of no account, with but feeble hands and insufficient means, revolutionary and impracticable visionaries and dreamers, set forth to find the fountain of that deadly river and to cleanse its polluted waters ere they should reach the unconquerable Pool.

THE GOVERNOR

THE Governor of the State at length had attained the goal of his ambition; he was Governor.

With utmost vigilance and an assiduity that knew neither nights nor holidays, the respectable citizen had gathered step by step all the goods and distinctions of this world.

He was Governor; and now that he was installed, after so much enterprise and toil, the days of his honor seemed idle. There was nothing to struggle for, and he became listless and, to tell the truth, more weary than ever before in all his laborious life.

This man, so noted for invariable aplomb, an invincible winner of every stake he played for, found himself now at a Barmecide banquet garnished with the apples of Sodom.

Thus far he had looked out upon the world from one point of view, or at most two — his own interests and conflicting interests. But a metaphysician should perhaps resolve them into one. Now that he was Governor and risen above such narrowness, having no more to gain and secure from loss, it occurred to him to relieve the tedium of his office by traveling about among his subjects and discovering what they were like. Just to amuse himself he traveled in disguise, with no insignia of his rank, in commoner clothes even than those he had worn since that long past time when he was an obscure and penniless struggler.

He saw and talked with all conditions of men, the humble, the proud, the rich and the poor. To his astonishment, he found that every one wished to be Governor of the State. Every one thought he was qualified for the office, and nearly every one that he merited it.

"What, then," said he, "must not the Governor of the State be a great man?"

"Well, now," answered all, "does not being Governor make him a great man?"

He had never looked at it in that light. But he was a sensible man withal; and perchance for the first time in his life of arduous endeavor he now had time for reflection, and a third point of view.

He gave over traveling, and entered upon the duties of his office. He exhausted himself in labors for his people; but never before had he found any labor half so delightful, half so satisfactory.

At the close of his term of office, yes, mark you well, at the end, when he was about to become a private citizen once more, all the people said he was a great man.

I SHOULD not write about pigmies, as it is so little a subject, except for the sake of controversy. Homer and some others who love to make small things large, and the large larger, contend that they are thirteen and one half inches in height. This I deny.

"But first let us have some premise, some *pou sto* to set out from." Well, I assert that there are such beings as pigmies, and second that they are men. "Agreed." Then I proceed: there are pigmies; pigmies are men; they are thirteen and one half inches in height. "It must be so." I admit the first two propositions, but deny the third; they are not thirteen and one half inches in height. "But that is mere assertion." Nay, I bring an eyewitness; I myself have seen them much smaller. "What confusion you introduce! This is not a court but a disputation. We want arguments, not facts. And are you speaking of pigmies, or men? I am completely confused." Both; I have seen pigmies who were men, and men much more dwarfed than pigmies.

But this is enough for so pigmean a subject.

IT was a great while ago that I set out to explore the world in order to better my condition and if possible exchange lots with some one more fortunate than myself.

In the world where I then had my being, this enterprise was not uncommon and seldom difficult, as the interchange took place between those who had everything to gain and nothing to lose. I demanded the same method, but on a more magnificent scale. And it seemed to me that I had something which all the world would want as soon as its existence was found out. On the other hand, I had heard of various possessions which I much desired for my own. I cannot remember now all of them, it was so long ago; and they were almost infinite in number, for at that time I never heard of any perfection that I did not immediately covet.

Fame, however, I do remember, was the first thing that made me acquisitive. Strangely enough it was an animal that kindled in me the ardor for fame. I was reading of Alexander and his war horse Bucephalus ; suddenly there came into my heart a feeling of emulation, of envy, not of Alexander but of Bucephalus, that he should be famous through so many ages, that even he should have had a city built and named in his honor on the stream of Hydaspes.

After that, all renowned works of men excited me beyond measure, and there was not one I did not feel equal to performing. I steadily looked forward to the doing something remarkable ; but it was always that which had already been done remarkably ; that which had been achieved and crowned. Ah, yes, it was the crown that dazzled. However, there is some merit, some nobleness in youth that is susceptible to such dazzling, and whose impetuosity will not stop to consider how long it takes for silver to become gold.

So I set forward to the conquest of the world on Bucephalus. It was a glorious morning, and a thousand omens beckoned me forward. The world seemed standing a-tiptoe to welcome me. Every one would be ready to exchange gifts, and I should soon possess all that I so ardently longed for. Hitherto longings had been more puissant than action in bringing the accomplishment of my aspirations. These are the pawns of the first years, craftily given away to lure us on.

Lightly I rode on toward the hill which had thus far bounded my horizon. For a long time I had supposed the world was just on the other side of that hill. Reaching the top, I looked up and down, but saw nothing — nothing save another hill beyond. It must be over there, I thought. I rode on. Still more hills, and higher and higher. After riding over these and many another, Bucephalus became worn out, and I was obliged to dismount and go on afoot, and I therefore threw away with infinite regret one after another those precious articles I had taken for my journey, which I thought would be much desired in the world to which I was going in triumph.

As I was now on foot, I avoided the hills that before had only seemed worthy of my steed and myself, and I began to traverse the valleys and plains. It was humiliating, but having lost Bucephalus and left behind most of my treasures, there was no help for it ; I had now only myself to recommend me, in case I should at length reach the world.

Wonderful to tell, it was in the

plains and valleys, and not as I supposed upon the glorious hilltops, that
I began to find signs of men — yes,
and not at all the sort of beings I had
imagined them.

"This," said I, "cannot after all be
the great world I have pictured. I will
inquire the way." Now before, this
had not seemed necessary, but only
just to ride on and one would surely
arrive.

"Why, here you are," answered a
man of whom I made my inquiry. "It
is right here; you need not take another step."

"Why," said I, "this is only what I
left behind — just like it."

"No doubt of it," answered the
man : "it's all of a piece; a common
sort of piece too, neither better nor
worse than what you see and will find
everywhere. What have you got to
sell ? "

"Nothing," said I.

"Well, then, what do you want to
buy ? "

"Nothing," I repeated.

"Ah, I see, you have made your fortune."

"On the contrary, I am in search of it, and that was the reason I was inquiring the way to the world."

"It is neither ahead of you nor behind you," now spoke the man, but rather less bluffly, I thought. "But what do you want of the world if you have nothing to sell and neither want to buy anything?"

"Oh," said I, "I understood the world was a place where one could exchange his own gifts for others which he desired. I heard of a great many which I deeply longed to have; and moreover, I felt sure that my own would be equally wanted, nay, indispensable, when once known."

"Young man," and now he spoke quite gravely, "I see you really have got your fortune to make, and you need not go a step further. Stay where you are. This is the world.

There is no more of it if you go round and over and through it. It is all of a piece, as I said, and common stuff at that; only remarkable when you do not know it very well, which I see is your case. Did you never learn of a place called Here, and a time called Now? You have arrived at both, and none too soon. Come, cast in your fortune with us, and you will find it. Be a brother of the common lot; Brethren of the Common Lot, we call ourselves in this corner of the world. and we are trying to extend the name. Perhaps you can help us. Do not think to better your lot except in the betterment of the common lot. Give what you have; expect nothing."

This was so different a reception to that I had anticipated that I was at first greatly chagrined and cast down. But the magnanimity of the man's appeal, when I came to reflect, appeared somehow so much akin to the early enthusiasm with which I set out on my pilgrimage, and in fact the clear echo of all those youthful and indistinct aspirations, that at length I yielded ; and contributing the few things I had managed to save, after Bucephalus gave out and I had left the ambitious hills, I became a regular and humble member of the Brethren of the Common Lot.

Sometimes now I see myself as at the beginning of my adventure, and I smile ; but poor Bucephalus sometimes makes me sigh. Whoever rides him is sure of a fall ; yet for all that wishes to mount again and resume the vision of a world led in triumphal procession.

Thus I dally often with the shining memorials of greatness ; but not for that Olympian dream would I now exchange the substantial happiness created for each other by magnanimous and sympathetic men.

I salute you, Brethren of the Common Lot ! Let me ever share your life ; and may I, in a little degree, increase your joys and lessen your sorrows.

THE SUPERFLUOUS MAN

THE excess of funds, of incomes or of productions, is nothing to be compared to a surplus man — the one more than is needed. It arrests the economy of the universe. He usually leads a melancholy life, or betimes commits suicide. But upon Peter Demeter the lot fell happily, and with success. Every one loved him, although nobody required his services. He was left entirely out of the account of worldly affairs, as much as if he were the creation of mythology, or of a poet's fancy. He had room for himself, space, in the astronomical sense, and that was all.

Wherever he proffered his services they were declined, not unkindly, but with a word and manner that implied he existed for other purposes. If he was found by his mistress helping the maids in the kitchen scour knives, she would say, " Peter, you need not do that ; Sarah has nothing else to do ; it is her work." Then Peter wandered into the garden, and seeing the weeds, began to pull them. But his master passing by said, " Now, Peter, do not trouble yourself about the weeds ; the gardener has men enough to look out for the garden."

It was just so at the barn, in the field, summer and winter. Everywhere his efforts were declined; it was another's work ; the place was filled.

At length it seemed to poor, superfluous Peter that this was his lot in life, that is, the man not needed, the one man too many in the company. Nevertheless, so long as he was not kicked out of the world, but had properly the empire of an empty place, the recognized lord of nothing-to-do, and as much beloved as if he had written three successful plays, or were the owner of a prize yacht, Peter Demeter contented himself with being instead of doing.

Philosophy, it is said, makes one resigned to his fortune, and Peter was a philosopher in his homely, unconscious way. Retiring to the oaks in warm afternoons he meditated much, and came to the conclusion that superior beings and powers were also without occupations. At least, it seemed to him that God did not lift a finger in the afternoon of pleasant summer days. In the morning and toward sundown there appeared to be some stir, but one could not call it work. It was more like the thought in his mind, which came and went, and then all was still again. In this stillness he heard that work had long since ceased; and that for a great many ages past, all, save man, had been existing in heavenly, undisturbed meditation and repose. Nature herself was simply being, without effort or labor.

At night when Peter looked up at those bright spots in the heavens, he was more than ever convinced that they existed like himself, there where nothing was expected of them but to be still and serenely shine.

In fine, he found that he was not alone in having nothing to do and in being only wanted for himself. There was God, and all infinite, divine things; the stars, and nature for the most part, in exactly the same predicament. Certainly, he was in good company, although he belonged not in any earthly society of doers and sufferers.

THE FAMILY MIRROR

Six generations and a half had seen themselves reflected in it. Children had raised themselves on tiptoe and stood on chairs to begin the lifelong search for themselves. Before it aged and spectacled women had for two centuries arranged their caps and bonnets — a little one-sided — and turned to a daughter's eyes for the last touch. Babies had been held in front of it, and had leaned from their mother's arms to welcome with a kiss the face seen for the first time. Dogs held up to its disinterested reflections growled at the intruding stranger; and cats, bewildered by the image of themselves in its obscure depths, ran off in terror.

The reflection of the walls of the room was two hundred years old, but in its impassive, unagitated projection upon the polished glass, it had not grown old at all nor ever wearied or worn its ancient vis-à-vis.

The mirror gleamed as brightly as on the first day it was hung in its place ; it had the same sincere counter-feit for every one who stopped before it, or only passed, never so much as turning the head. But that was rarely. Or, if it happened so, it was with such ·as had become negligent of them-selves, or indifferent to the opinions of others. Or, it might be one — and that was the only time the mirror's hospitable heart was dimmed with jealousy — one who hurried by to see herself mirrored in the eyes of her lover.

The room in which it hung was alone its loyal, eternal companion. "We have been together a long time," said the mirror. "So much is changed ; so many are gone we used to see ; so many new faces before me. No sooner have I seen them grow up and become fond of displaying their beauty before me, which I had the joy of first telling them of, than I begin to discover wrinkles and furrows, the roses of their cheek and lip pale, waving hair straighten and whiten, and the jaws droop from the toothless mouth. I conceal these as long as I can, but, alas, they are on some day discovered, and the dejected creatures come no more to me for flattery. They come only to know they yet live and must put on their clothes as usual. Then in pity I help them to pin a collar in its place, or to see that a waist is not under the arms."

Six generations and a half had come and gone in the family mirror, and notwithstanding its complaint their images sometimes returned and presented themselves in its faithful face. It had kept in the strictest confidence all the family secrets. It had seen the blemishes as well as the forbidden charms of many a maiden beauty. It had seen without a blush upon its chaste face the nude, the *décolleté*, the common dishabille. Its pudicity and secrecy were articles of faith among the women of the family. Else why those planetary rings of skirts in the middle of the floor, still warm from the so lately cinctured star? Why those jewels scattered with so lavish hands; those slippers walking in so many and in such contrary directions; those powders, perfumes, brushes and combs and pins, ribbons and laces, all the delenda and indusiæ of past festival toilets; all that bewildering, captivating confusion? No, never had the loyal mirror betrayed these confidences. It had only amused itself with such foibles; it remained familiar, and dissembled its experiences with ladies like a successful courtier.

But it was quite another emotion when with high ancestral pride it mirrored and was honored with a parting glance from the family's latest bride.

A tear ran down its usually placid and imperturbable countenance.

What fashions in dress had it not seen! what beauty, what sweetness of mouth and of eye grow to their zenith, then descend to decay! It had even looked upon the face of the dead when taken down to testify if any breath yet lingered to tarnish its silvery, polished surface. It treasured in its deepest heart innumerable records of vanity, of love and hate which had been unwittingly revealed to it, and which it learned to know almost at the first look. These it sent away from its presence, confident of not being discovered by any one else; while all the outward fashion of face and form it sent away in equal confidence of being disclosed and admired by everybody.

It never itself practiced any kind of deceit, though often the witness of self-deception, and six generations and a half, fondly in youth and sadly in old age, had believed all that it revealed to them. Nor had it ever grown old, though seeing so many years, so many families appear, disappear and reappear. It shone as brightly as ever in its ancient oaken frame, adorned with gilded rosettes and reticulations of niello. There was but one mark of the abusive years, but one blemish in all its luminous surface, a small spot that reflected — nothing! Through that spot a boy of the sixth generation had once undeceived himself, and all his illusions had fled away. He too curiously sought the mirror's secret ; and lo, removing the enchanted silver curtain, astonished and suddenly, prematurely wise, penetrating the mystery, he looked through the hypocritic glass and found nothing there — found neither the substantial image of himself for which he was in search, nor a single one of those shadows which had seen themselves in it for two hundred years.

A MOUNTAIN MAID

Among the mountains the eyes are uplifted and acquire the habit of psalmists and preachers. From their pinnacles one again seeks the level of his being, and sees more distinctly whither the stream of his life is flowing, or where it stagnates. A stage-coach is the happy medium of contemplation; its elevation is not too great; one still looks up, but down also. Whatever is below is but slightly diminished; the loftiness of nature and the littleness of man are abridged; the passenger still feels an interest in earthly things.

I looked down into the upturned eyes of a little maid by the roadside, who mutely offered a cup of strawberries. Their fragrance exhaled toward me as freshly as when I have bent over them in the grass. She herself seemed like

the flower from which they had grown
— child of the forest and the mountain
pasture. Untamed as yet, her eyes
had the gleam of an animal, uncertain
whether you are friendly or hostile.
Not one suave, fawning taint had she
of the beggar who solicits or the seller
who sells. Take them or leave; she
invites you only as the strawberry on
the stem invites you to pluck and eat.
She has no want that you can supply;
and any small coin will fill her cup,
when you have taken and eaten, as
full as it was before — full, to over-
flowing. And she will not be grateful; there is a deeper, richer feeling
than that in her little heart — it re-
joices and leaps up. Her happiness
is her own; it does not concern you,
nor are you the cause of it. You are
merely coincident, you the accidental
spectator.

I look down into her unconquerable eyes, in whose hazel depths sleeps
the spirit that controls her being, and

which will be self-discovered in long years of suffering and thought, or in an instant of joy. She knows not yet that her feet are bare; their customary brown does not abash her; nor her tanned hands, nor the ends of her fingers pink only with the wine of the strawberry, nor her short frock whose barbaric calico her white apron half conceals. I cannot tell whether her lips are a natural color or painted with strawberries; but much should I like to put them to the test. But she, the untamable, the imperious maid, would rather be struck than caressed. Her nature, as yet sexless, admonishes her of the beginnings of the loss of freedom. Her foot is light on the trap that will subdue her.

I reach down for the cup of strawberries while she on tiptoe holds it up, and there is a sudden gleam in her eyes as if she read my thoughts and defied their familiarity.

I ride on, and I think of thee, little

queen of thy native mountains, as I
see peak after peak whose heights
threaten while they attract ; where
man can never build his house nor
bring his bride until worn — worn to
the common level.

THE DIVIDED HOUSE

THE mountain once looked down upon it with sympathy. For before Capella began to climb over the Moats, Chocorua itself was nearly rent in twain. But it healed the chasm with the forests, and made of the rent a pathway to the stars.

For millions of years the mountain beheld neither men nor houses at its feet. At length it saw approach, hand in hand, a human pair. It saw a house builded. Then to Chocorua the veil was lifted ; the meaning of the world, the long silence, its own solitude and wounds, the interminable periods of the creative forge, were revealed. With such joy did it watch toward the earth that it lost half its height, and forgot its ancient neighbor the sky.

Capella arose slowly and sorrowfully

with an uncertain gleam, hovering in
the tops of the pines.   In midsummer
the leaves of the vine turned their
backs to the bitter north wind.   The
butterfly folded her wings and remained motionless.   The brooks hid
themselves among the stones, the
Lake shrank to a puny bowl.

Chocorua, astonished at these things,
looked down into the valley and saw
the beloved house cut into two parts
by the same hands that had planned
and built.   Exactly through the centre
went axe and saw.   He took his half,
she hers ; and facing each other, with
lone, unclasped hands, they now made
the sundered sides the very fronts of
their separate dwellings.

There they lived out their lives,
defiantly but without speech, until the
windows were dark ; and the ruins of
that divided house the traveler jour-
neying toward the mountain still sees
and questions.

But never again did Chocorua take

any pleasure in the affairs of men and women. It withdrew; it raised itself once more to its ancient heights, its primeval thoughts. And this is why, disappointed with mankind, it is to-day so haughty, so mysterious and incommunicable.